© Finn Ståle Felberg

PER PETTERSON's *I Curse the River of Time* won the 2009 Nordic Council Literature Prize, the 2008 Norwegian Critics Prize, and the 2008 Brage Prize, and has become an international bestseller. His novel *Out Stealing Horses* has been translated into more than forty languages and won the International IMPAC Dublin Literary Award, the largest international prize for a work of fiction written in any language and published in English. *Out Stealing Horses* was also named a Best Book of 2007 by *The New York Times, Time, Entertainment Weekly,* and many other publications. Petterson is the author of six novels, including *In the Wake* and *To Siberia*. He was born in Oslo to a working-class family and lives in Norway.

DON BARTLETT lives in England and works as a freelance translator of Scandinavian literature. He has translated or co-translated Norwegian novels by Lars Saabye Christensen, Roy Jacobsen, Ingvar Ambjørnsen, Kjell Ola Dahl, Gunnar Staalesen, Pernille Rygg, and Jo Nesbø.

Per Petterson

It's Fine by Me

TRANSLATED FROM THE NORWEGIAN
BY

Don Bartlett

Picador   New York

IT'S FINE BY ME. Copyright © 1992 by Forlaget Oktober, Oslo. English translation copyright © 2011 by Don Bartlett. All rights reserved. Printed in the United States of America. For information, address Picador, 175 Fifth Avenue, New York, N.Y. 10010.

www.picadorusa.com
www.twitter.com/picadorusa • www.facebook.com/picadorusa
picadorbookroom.tumblr.com

Picador® is a U.S. registered trademark and is used by St. Martin's Press under license from Pan Books Limited.

For book club information, please visit www.facebook.com/picadorbookclub or e-mail marketing@picadorusa.com.

Picador ISBN 978-0-312-59534-0

Picador books may be purchased for educational, business, or promotional use. For information on bulk purchases, please contact Macmillan Corporate and Premium Sales Department at 1-800-221-7945, extension 5442, or write specialmarkets@macmillan.com.

Originally published in Great Britain by Harvill Secker, a division of Random House Group Ltd, London

First published in the United States by Graywolf Press

First Picador Edition: October 2013

10   9   8   7   6   5   4   3   2   1

I

1

I was thirteen years old and about to start the seventh class at Veitvet School. My mother said she would go with me on the first day – we were new to the area, and anyway she had no job – but I didn't want her to. It was the 18th of August, the sky was all grey, and as I opened the school gate and went into the playground, it started to rain. I pushed my sunglasses up my nose and walked slowly across the open expanse. It was deserted. Midway, I stopped and looked around. To the right there were two red prefabs, and straight ahead lay the squat, blue main building. And there was a flagpole with a wet, heavy flag clinging to the halyard. Through the windows I could see faces, and those sitting on the inside pressed their noses against the panes and watched me standing in the rain. It was bucketing down. It was my first day, and I was late.

By the time I reached the entrance, my hair was streaming and my shirt was soaking wet. I took it off and wrung it hard and wiped the sunglasses on my jeans before I put them back, and I pulled my shirt over my head. Then I went in.

The first thing I saw was the Norwegian Constitution. It was on the wall, behind glass, just to the right. The second thing was the headmaster's office. There was no mistaking it, because there was a sign on the door. I headed straight for that sign without slackening my pace in case someone was watching me, and I would hate to make them think I didn't know where I was going. I knocked and stared straight at the door while I was waiting, and when a voice shouted 'COME IN!', I opened the door and did not look to either side.

It was a large room with shelving along the walls, a spirit duplicator in a corner and a desk. Behind the desk sat a large, rather fat man. He raised his head from a pile of papers and looked me over. Through the sunglasses it was hard to see if he was smiling, but I don't believe he was.

'The tops of your boots,' he said. I looked down. Like everybody else I wore brown rubber boots folded down over my calves and on the lining I had written BEATLES in block capitals. I crouched and turned them up.

'I can't think of anything I dislike more,' he said.

I shrugged and waited. He sat eyeing me and there was a long silence before he said:

'Now take off your sunglasses. I like to know who I'm talking to.'

I shook my head.

'You won't?'

I shook my head again.

'May I ask why?' His face was a balloon, a moon with dark patches.

'I have scars.'

'Scars?'

'Terrible scars round my eyes.'

'Is that so?' He slowly nodded with that round head of his and stroked his chin. 'May I have a look?'

'No.'

'No?' He was lost for words. He drummed a pencil. 'Well, what's your name then?'

'Audun Sletten. I'm supposed to begin the seventh class here.'

'I see, so you're Audun Sletten, are you? I've been waiting half an hour for you.'

'I got lost.'

'You got lost?'

'Yes.'

'Is that possible? There's only one way down here, isn't there?'

I shrugged. He felt unsure now. I knew he could not see my eyes. I was the Phantom. He sighed and stood up.

'You'll be starting in the B class. It's mixed. We have a girls' class, a boys' class and a mixed class in the seventh year. Follow me.'

He walked towards the door with small, quick steps, even though he was a big man, and heavy, like John Wayne, slightly knock-kneed, and I jumped to the side so he could pass, and then we were in the corridor. I trudged after him. Compared with the school I used to go to, this one seemed never-ending. Halfway down the corridor he stopped and turned.

'Are you sure those scars are so terrible?'

'They're so goddamn terrible,' I said. His hand moved towards my glasses and I took one step back and raised my fists. It was instinctive. Then he lowered his hands.

'You'd better mind your language,' he said, 'we don't want any swearing here.'

I said nothing, and we walked to the very end of the corridor where he stopped, knocked on a door and opened it, not waiting for an answer. He held it open and waved me in. They all looked at us. One girl giggled. I sensed him breathing down my neck and braced myself in case he should try anything stupid.

'This is Audun Sletten, the new boy I'm sure you have heard about. He's come to us from the countryside so please give him a warm welcome. He, too, likes the Beatles. Don't mind the sunglasses. They're glued to his nose.'

The girl giggled again. She had black hair down to her shoulders. Before leaving he stooped and whispered in my ear.

'I will call your mother about the scars, don't you worry.'

'We don't have a telephone,' I said aloud, but by then he was gone.

'Well not everybody has one,' the teacher said, 'but thank you for telling us.' Half the class laughed.

'You can have the vacant desk by the window.' He had gold-framed glasses, his hair was thinning at the front, but he looked as if he kept in shape because his shirt was tight round his chest and his biceps. I walked in front of the class, past the dais and along the row and sat down at the desk by the window. I hung my bag on the hook at the side. It had stopped raining. The sun cut through the clouds and the light turned the playground into a lake, and there were rafts on the shiny water, and fishing rods and a dam like the one up by Lake Aurtjern, and you could stand there and cast your line where the fish hugged the rocks. As I turned to face the blackboard everything went dark and it took some time before I could see through my sunglasses what was written there in chalk. *WELCOME!* it said. I ducked under the desk and folded my boots down again.

The bell rang and I was the last to leave, I didn't want anyone at my back. The teacher's name was Levang. He wanted to shake hands and be nice, so I shook his hand and mumbled something even I couldn't make out, and headed off. I crossed to the other side of the playground and leaned against the wire mesh. There was a football pitch beyond the fence, but it was deserted now, the dark shale steaming. To the right of me by the prefabs, kids were chasing each other, playing tag and splashing water. To the left, by the main building, the older ones were standing in clusters talking. A few girls were skipping rope, and coming straight towards me was a boy on crutches. I had seen him in the classroom, on the right, a little closer to the blackboard. I glanced left and right, but there was no one else by the fence. He had dark, curly hair and boots like mine, with KINKS written on the one and HOLLIES on the other. They were English pop groups, but I did not have any of their records. I did not have any records at all. We just had Jussi Björling, the Swedish opera singer, although I did have a transistor radio that I listened to in the night.

He stopped a few metres away from me, leaned on his crutches and smiled.

'Cool shades,' he said.

Cool crutches, I thought, but I didn't say it. They *were*

cool in a way, like an extra part of his body he took with him everywhere, he didn't even notice, they were just there.

'I'll be rid of them in two months,' he said, following my gaze. 'I've had them for a year. They don't bother me now, but I can't wait.'

'What's wrong with your leg?'

'Car accident.'

'So what happened to the car?'

He laughed so much he almost fell off his crutches.

'I don't know. I didn't see it. Someone drove into me from behind, and I blacked out and woke up in my grandmother's spare room.' He laughed again, his whole face smiling. 'When I woke up, I thought I was in heaven, because the first thing I saw was one of those pictures where it says *Jesus lives*.'

'So you believe in God then?'

'No, I never have, but when I woke up in my grandmother's house, I thought perhaps I'd been wrong. Luckily then, I worked out where I was. That picture had always been there.'

He leaned on his crutches, dangling one leg over the grip and laughed non-stop. I had decided not to make friends with anyone at this school, but this bloke was hard to refuse.

'Something wrong with your eyes?'

'I can't take the bright light,' I said and felt bad about it, because that wasn't quite true, but it was truer than other things I had said. 'I start throwing up straight away.'

'Fair enough,' he said, and there was a silence, and I felt like a fraud. But then a ball rolled our way. I saw it first and was going to give it a kick, but then he saw it too, got ready, and using his crutches as a pommel horse, he thumped the ball with his good leg so hard it flew to the other end of the playground and smacked into the fence. It was impressive, but not something you did on a football field.

'Not bad,' I said, and he just kept on grinning and said: 'My name's Arvid, by the way,' and then the bell rang.

This time it was easier to enter the classroom, I was not the last one in, but I kept my glasses on. As long they left me in peace, this day might be OK.

When we were all seated at our desks, Levang went up to the dais and sat down as well, crossed his hands and let his gaze wander around the class until it settled on me. He smiled, I felt my neck go stiff, and then he said in a very friendly voice:

'Well, Audun. There wasn't much time in the first lesson, but now I was wondering if maybe you could tell us something about what it's like where you come from. Most of the class, you know, haven't lived anywhere else but here in Veitvet. What's it called, the place where you grew up?'

I should have known. He wasn't going to leave me in peace. He was a nice man, no doubt about it, and he was doing this for my sake, he wanted me to feel at home. I shrugged.

'I mean, it could be interesting for us to hear about. Did you live on a farm?'

'There's nothing to tell,' I said in a loud voice. The black-haired girl was giggling again.

Levang smiled, his face slightly flushed. 'Surely that can't be true,' he said. 'I mean, you're thirteen years old, after all. You must have experienced lots of things that are different from what we are used to here.'

'I said there's nothing to tell!'

'Are you sure?' he asked. Then I got up from the desk, grabbed my schoolbag from the hook on the side and made for the door. No one was giggling now.

Arvid turned to look at me, but his eyes told me nothing of what was in his mind.

'Oi, where are you going?' Levang said, and then he got up and took a few steps to cut me off. I felt my whole body tense up. I looked past his shoulder to the door, but there was no point in trying.

'I've always done my homework,' I said. 'I've always paid attention. You can see my school report if you like, but you have no right to ask me questions about things that have nothing to do with school.'

'Whoa there, Audun, I think you've got the wrong end of the stick. I didn't mean it like that,' he said and tried to catch my eye, but I was looking right past his ear and didn't answer.

'Well, let's talk about this some other time. Please would you go to your desk now.' I turned and walked back down between the desks. I took a quick glance at Arvid's face, and then I sat down and hung up my bag and stared out of the window.

II

2

Autumn has come, and I am on my newspaper round. Jimi Hendrix just died, they are playing 'Hey Joe' on the radio, and I have passed my driving test. I have my reefer jacket on, a pair of checked flares and a broad, red plaited belt with a loop buckle. Down the flare from the knee is a row of shiny buttons. It's the latest fashion, and if anyone had seen me I would have really stood out. But not many people are up, only a lamp in the odd window, and as I walk the hills up from the block where I live towards the depot in the shopping centre, it's a quarter past five. There is a frozen silver sheen on the lawns between the rows of terraced houses, and it's not yet morning. I have had my hair cut in a moderate-mod style after several years of long hair, and I am not sure it's such a big hit. So the gloom suits me fine.

I am tired, I still have homework to do and a sinking feeling in the pit of my stomach tells me something at school is not going the right way. What I do, I do well enough. What I hear, I remember and understand, I am not an idiot, but it's as if the rest of my class has taken off on some journey they forgot to tell me about, as if there is a secret pact between teacher and students that does not include me. They know something I do not, and that's how it has been for a long time now.

The others stand waiting in front of the entrance, I am the last to turn up, but there are no newspapers in sight. Konrad is there, and Fru Johansen, and the entire Vilden family, the two children yawning and leaning against their father's back. This is what they live off, four newspaper rounds morning and afternoon, day in, day out. The oldest child, a girl, is fourteen years old, the boy twelve. They look as though they have just come out of the forest, you'd expect pine needles in their hair, but they live in Rådyrveien, in a flat, like the rest of us from Veitvet do. The mother is so ugly and bony that you *have* to like her, and the father, tall and distant, nods politely to the left, right and centre, and never says a word, just smiles and looks over our heads at something we don't quite comprehend. High plains and spruce forests, I have always imagined. The girl is so attractive it's hard to look her in the face.

'Hi, Audun,' says the boy called Tommy, and I say:

'Hi Tommy, cool jacket.' We often talk, I lend him old Cowboy and Indian books, and we are pals. He always seems to have a cold, a red patch under his nose, and he wears a striped, yellow jacket lined with fur and smiles happily, even though he has had the jacket on all week, and I have said 'cool jacket' every morning. I don't talk to his sister, her eyes are so big and brown that after walking the same route for several years I still don't know her name. But she looks at my new trousers.

We wait. It's the third day in a row that the newspapers are late. Konrad's moped is chugging away on its stand, he doesn't switch it off unless he has to and burns up a hell of a lot of petrol. He already wears a cap, a grey bobble cap

14

without a bobble that he pulls down so hard his ears stick out, like the retarded kids you see in town sometimes, and you wonder why they have to dress them like that. He has woollen gloves on with the fingers cut off, and his fingers are black with the old ink. He is fifty years old and lives with his sister in the terraced house right across from the women's prison, and no one can wedge a newspaper behind a door handle like him. In one flowing movement his hand makes an arc in mid-air and the fat *Aftenposten* is lodged under the handle as hard as a board and never comes loose. How easy it looks, and yet I have tried it many times, and I cannot do it.

We hear the car before we see it, it's the only sound there is apart from Konrad's moped, and at full speed it sails up the incline from Veitvetveien, makes a U-turn in front of the depot and comes to a stop by our barrows. The driver jumps out, yanks the side doors back and hauls out the big bundles of newspapers. He drops them on the tarmac, with a loud groan each time, thwack, thwack they go, hitting the ground with a solid thud I've always thought had something to do with what is in the newspapers.

I pull out my two bundles and load them on to the barrow, cut the strings and check to see if there are any new subscribers. There are: two. I enter their names in my book and start dragging the barrow towards Grevlingveien. The others set off on their separate routes. Konrad up to Trondhjemsveien, Fru Johansen along Beverveien, which is where I live, and the Vilden family down to the houses along Rådyrveien. Tommy is carrying a huge bundle of papers. As usual he has cut the strings first, and now the papers start slipping and sliding in his arms, and the whole caboodle is on the verge of crashing to the ground. His sister comes over, bends down to give a hand, and they are so wonderful to watch it takes my breath away, but I too have siblings. One brother and a sister. That is, I had a brother. Last year he drove a Volvo Amazon that did not belong to him into the river Glomma and drowned. It happened just a few miles from where we used to live before we moved to Veitvet. It was an Amazon with all the extras: fox tail on the aerial, GT steering wheel and fur-lined seat covers at the front.

The girl in the passenger seat survived. She wept and said they hadn't touched a drop. I don't believe that for one moment. Egil had just turned fifteen the autumn before and didn't have a licence yet. After we moved to Oslo he went back as often as he could when he was old enough to go alone. I didn't. I only go there when I have to.

My sister moved out just after the accident. She is four years older than me, and of course she too had to go back. Now she lives with her boyfriend in Kløfta. He sells second-hand cars and makes money. I am sure he beats her, but I have never seen anything, and Kari does not say a word. If ever I catch him I'll beat *him* up. That won't cost me much. I have been training for years. With my newspaper money I bought a bench and weights.

I tell my mother.

'I'll give him a *thrashing*,' I say. And she listens to me and then she quotes Lars Ekborg, the Swede who has a talk show on the radio where he goes on and on about all kinds of shit happening in the world and always rounds off by saying: 'You've got to be tough, you really do!'

'Is that how you want it?' she laughs. Sure, it's easy to make fun, but I know what I know.

I remember Egil and me playing on the living-room floor in our old house. There was a massive cupboard we used to crawl under. My grandfather, who worked at the sawmill in the next village, had made it himself out of some dark wood and there were glass doors. It was a fine cupboard, his greatest achievement, but it must have drained his creativity, for he never made a piece of furniture again.

Then my father came in. It was late, and we should have been in bed by then. He leaned against the door frame and looked at us with a stupid smile on his face.

'Are there any good children here?' he slurred. He seemed drunk. I had seen him drunk many times before. I knew the signs.

'Oh yes,' Egil said, crawling out from under the cupboard where he had been hiding. He was such an idiot, he would have said yes to anything. I sat on the floor and watched my father leaning heavily against the door frame. I did not trust him.

He straightened up and staggered towards us across the carpet.

'See this,' he said, and shoved his hand into his breast pocket and pulled out some banknotes. 'Here's a little something for two good boys.' He stumbled forward with a big grin and pushed a blue five-kroner note at each of us.

'Oh, thank you, thank you,' Egil cried, and started running round and jumping up and down on the floor. 'Oh, thank you very, very much, Dad, you're so kind!' he shouted. I felt the crisp crackle of the note in my hand. Five kroner was a lot of money to me. Just a little more, with what I had already saved up, and it would be enough to buy the shiny bow I had looked at so many times in the sports shop by the station.

I watched my father standing in the middle of the floor with his hands on his hips and his head at an angle. He didn't look so drunk now, he was watching us closely and there was a glint in his eye I did not like. Suddenly he burst into laughter, and then his face froze, he came back across the floor and snatched the notes from our hands and said:

'That's enough fun for tonight!' He turned on his heel without a stagger, stuffed the notes back in his breast pocket and marched to the kitchen as straight as a flagpole. 'Now, get to bed, it's late,' he said.

At first my brother stood with his mouth wide open, then he began to howl like the baby he was. 'Waaaah!' he wailed. 'Waaah!' Tears gushed from his eyes, and I went over to him and punched him in the shoulder.

'You idiot,' I said, punching him hard a second time. 'You goddamn birdbrain, shut up!' I hissed, and then I walked past him on my way upstairs to bed.

'I never did anything to you!' he yelled after me.

It was my last year as Wata, Davy Crockett's friend of the Creek tribe. As soon as I was on my own, I was Wata. I was twelve years old, and I went up the squeaking stairs to the

18

first floor of what I thought of as our log cabin, and I hated it now, it felt so cramped I could not breathe.

Inside our room, I stood by the window gazing out at the dark edge of the forest, longing to be there. There were paths running through it I knew better than the house I lived in. That night there was a moon, big and yellow, and I lingered and kept watch as Wata would have done, and then I got into bed without cleaning my teeth and hoped that Egil would not be up before I had gone to sleep. I pinched my eyes shut and thought of the shiny bow I would never have.

'Shit!' I said aloud in the darkness. 'You goddamn pale-face!' But that did not help much, and I knew that Wata's days were numbered. He could not be my companion any longer. I saw him glide through the night, fleet-footed and silent through the trees on his way back into the books, his brown body and his three white feathers gleaming in the moonlight.

Now Tommy has his newspapers under control, his sister gives him a hug, the yellow stripes of his jacket shining, and they disappear round a corner. I take twenty papers from the barrow, fold them under my arm and start working my way along the first houses in Grevlingveien. This is what I like. To be left in peace, feel the morning air on my face, feel every step, how my arms and legs move, and the morning so still, and I don't have to think about anything. My round goes like clockwork, the shining door handles line up and I feed them with newspapers. I have never missed a single one, never given anyone a paper they shouldn't have, and I know every door sign so well that at first I don't even remember what they say, just what they look like, the shape of the letters, the colours and where on the door they are. I can think of a house, picture it, choose that door and *then* read the sign any time, anywhere, asleep in bed, at school, on holiday, it's in my bones, and that's fine with me.

I cross Veitvetsvingen down by the red telephone kiosk. I have a quick look under the grate on the floor to see if any change has fallen through, a habit I guess I'll never quit, and as always I find two or three kroner. But I blush and hope there is no one watching me from behind their curtains.

There are only terraced houses along the road, and a few years ago I thought maybe it was posher to live here rather than in the tenement blocks, until I realised that the blocks were just two terraced houses on top of each other, and inside they were identical. At the bottom of the hill, on the left, there is a terrace of eight flats. Arvid lives in the one next to last. It's the only house with balconies, and in the old days Arvid was nervous it would make him upper class, because nobody we knew lived in a house with a balcony. But I didn't reckon three and a half square metres of balcony was enough to make him upper class, especially since his father worked night shifts at the Jordan brush factory. Arvid was happy to hear that. Under no circumstances did he want to be upper class, and as far as that goes, we both stand firm.

I walk up the flagstone path and round the back of Arvid's

house. There are four subscribers here. His father is not among them, but as I pass I stop at the kitchen window and peer in. It's dark inside, so he is not home from the night shift yet. I turn at the end of the house and on to the road again, and look up at Arvid's window on the first floor, pick up a pebble and throw it against the pane. I hear it hit the glass and Arvid is there at once. I don't know anyone who's such a light sleeper, and he is often tired at school. He sticks out his dark head, I roll up a newspaper tight and skim it at an angle like a boomerang, and it makes a perfect arc, and Arvid snatches it out of the air before it hits the window frame. We have done this before.

'Latest news from Vietnam,' I say.

'I guess they're bombing Hanoi again.' He yawns and runs his hand through his hair which is curly and very thick.

'You bet,' I say. Arvid is in the National Liberation Front group at school. He can go on for hours about it. I am a passive member, I have too many other things on my mind.

'I'll read it later,' he says, 'I have stuff to do. I've got to go.'

'What sort of stuff?'

'You'll see it when you see it.'

'See you at school,' I say and he salutes me with a clenched fist behind the window. I walk towards the barrow and then turn on my heel, but he is gone and I grab the handle and trudge round the bend back towards Grevlingveien.

Morning is coming, but there is not much light yet, it's October, after all, and the early risers are coming down the road towards the Metro. I say hello and one of them looks at my hair and another one at my trousers and is annoyed

21

because I am late, but I splay my hands and say it's not my fault, and then a few papers tumble to the ground. The man looks up, rolls his eyes, and I mutter a silent curse.

Old Abrahamsen comes out on to the step and angrily slams the door behind him. Every day he does this and has done so for as long as I can remember. He works at the harbour and is carrying his rucksack. He used to live in Vika, not far from where he worked, straight out of the door, past Oslo West station and there he was, but they demolished Vika and now he has to travel into town every morning, and even though it's fifteen years since he had to move, he is still fuming. The Metro is too newfangled, so he walks up Trondhjemsveien and takes the number 30 bus as he has been doing for almost two decades.

'Hi,' I say. 'Just in time for the paper – read it on the bus,' and he smiles and says:

'Well, you know, *Aftenposten* is really not my thing, but you have to keep up to date.'

I know, he is a socialist, but he is so stingy he has literally weighed the *Aftenposten* and the left-wing *Arbeiderbladet* and found that with *Aftenposten* he gets more kilos for his money. He puts the paper under his arm and all of a sudden is a much happier man and is off down the road, the rucksack bumping on his back.

I am seriously late now and pick up the pace and stop greeting people. The road narrows, the last houses are at the edge of Dumpa, where Condom Creek flows through, and on the other side, the ground rises in a steep arch up to the women's prison at the top. Heavy and sombre, it faces Groruddalen valley and the ribbon of morning light that's stealing in over Furuset, and only a solitary lamp burns in the prison courtyard. It seems cold, the light, and I go cold myself, for the mere thought of so many women locked in behind those thick walls is painful, and I wonder what they recall when they wake up in the morning, what they speak about over dinner, what they think about when they go to bed at night. I picture people in chains, and know it's not like that, but what do they see when they look out the windows?

Fru Karlsen is standing on the steps as I come round the corner to the very last house. She is smiling and I know she has been waiting for me. She often does. She is holding an envelope in her hand, and when I pass her the newspaper she puts the envelope in my jacket pocket and says: 'I was away for your birthday, you know, but better late than never. Many happy returns.'

I didn't know she had been away, but she has found out when my birthday is and made a point of remembering it and now she is giving me a present. It feels awkward. Only my mother gives me birthday presents and that's the way it's always been. And then this lady. She smells nice. She can't be a day over forty, she's good-looking, too. I feel my pulse racing, and the words I was going to say fall back into my mouth and are gone. But she smiles and has a good look at my checked trousers and my hair and smiles even more and then she strokes my cheek before she closes the door. My cheek burns and I am not able to say thank you, or anything else for that matter, just stand there looking at the door where it says *Karlsen*. I know she has a husband, but I have never seen him. He is probably an idiot. The heat from my face spreads down my neck to my chest.

I open the envelope and there is a hundred-kroner note inside. Hell, a hundred kroner, that's too much. My legs start to itch, I have to get out of here. I dare not turn round. She might be standing behind the curtains watching, maybe expecting some sign from me.

Grevlingveien is a dead end street, but a footpath at the end leads up to Trondhjemsveien, alongside the Metro track. I leave the barrow and walk up far enough to be out of Fru Karlsen's sight and lean against the wire mesh fence by the path, take the tobacco from my jacket, roll a cigarette and light it. Behind the fence the hill rises sharply, and there is a white house on the top where the prison governor lives, and the fields beneath have always had that smell of burnt withered grass in the spring. Now they smell of damp and mould. I shudder and take a deep drag and after a while I feel better. But a hundred kroner, that's not good.

I finish my cigarette and kill it with my shoe on the gravel, shoot a glance up towards Trondhjemsveien before I have to go back down, and there he is. There are maybe thirty metres between us, and I have not seen him for five years. But I know him at once. The black hair, the snappy black suit he seems to have slept in, the nondescript grey shirt without a tie. His suntanned neck and grey stubble; the unnaturally blue eyes I can't make out just now, but I know they're looking at me without even blinking. I cannot move, and he is standing stock still. I try to think, but nothing comes to mind, and he takes two steps down the footpath, and then I shout:

'STOP!' He stops, grabs the straps of his rucksack and waits. He is so dark, and as slim as a blade and not like anything else. Behind him, I can see the high-rises in Rødtvet and behind them just the forest and more forest and I know that's where he has come from. Had I been standing close to him now, I would have caught the smell of bonfire and pine trees and tobacco, and something more that could only be him. But I'm not standing close, and he scratches his chin, shakes his head, and I realise he hasn't recognised me until now. That's no surprise. I am much taller than when I was thirteen, I wear different clothes and my hair is different. He raises his hand as if to salute me, like an Indian would, and walks on a few paces, and I'm almost certain he's smiling.

'NOT ONE MORE STEP!' I shout. 'WHAT THE HELL ARE YOU DOING HERE? GO AWAY!' I raise my clenched fists, and my body tells me I am stronger than him. He stops, resting his hands on his hips and tips his head to the side in a pose I know so well, and it always unsettled me, which is what it's supposed to do. I stand with my fists in the air, and maybe he too feels unsettled. At any rate he turns and heads back for the main road, and I stay there until I am certain he has gone, and only then do I hurry down, back to the houses. I'm just a few steps along the footpath when I hear his laughter, and it makes my blood run cold. I cannot restrain myself and break into a run.

3

I cross Trondhjemsveien, walk past the church at Grorud and down the hills. I took the Metro today, I didn't want to walk the whole way, I couldn't do it. I sat all the way up looking straight ahead of me. My neck is aching, and still it's a long walk. Something growing in my chest makes me short of breath, forcing me to swallow again and again, but it doesn't help. I gaze into the cemetery where Egil is buried. It's hard to walk past without stopping, but when I do, I don't know what to think about him being dead. Like I always do, I stand there with my mind going blank and a wave of heat rushing up from my legs. I walk down the hill and it's as if someone is staring at me from behind.

I have changed my checked flares for regular Wranglers. I didn't have to, but still, it's a relief.

I come down the hill on to the brow and the narrow valley opens up and branches off onto Østre Aker vei, and just ahead of me is the yellow school building right by Grorud railway station and Grorud ironware factory barely visible behind the hillock to the left. On the other side of the railway line, there are the star-shaped houses where many of my classmates live: May Brit, Bente and Bente and Henrik. Their fathers are train drivers, or something else to do with the railway, and they all know each other. The school is at the bottom of the valley, and, to the left, beneath the cliff, the teachers live in their terraced houses, and a few writers too: Tor Obrestad, Einar Økland and Paal-Helge Haugen. Like birds on a wire, they sit in their windows looking up to the sky with the sun on their faces, holding on to the secret, and I envy them so furiously it makes my legs tremble. I have Haugen's *Anne* in my rucksack. It's like nothing else. So far, Gorky has been my hero, *My Childhood* the book above books, but Anne is lying there, in the book, seeing herself and the world through a haze of fever, and I can't get her out of my head, it makes me think about when I was thirteen, in bed with yellow fever in a house I hated more than anything else.

There is a cold wind blowing through Groruddalen, a constant blast of air all the way from the sea right up to Gjelleråsen Ridge, sweeping along Trondhjemsveien, chilling Østre Aker vei, and even the toughest boy wears a cap in winter to keep his ears from freezing to glass. It's still only October, but I am shivering where I stand looking almost right down into the schoolyard. The flag is flying though I can't imagine why. A gust of wind comes and unfurls it and I laugh out loud because the flag is red and blue with a large yellow star in the centre, it's a rebel flag, it gives me a jolt just to see it there, and from where I am standing it's clear that the halyard has been cut. If they want the flag taken down, they'll have to climb the pole first. I hurry down the last hill.

Down in the schoolyard, I see Arvid standing alone in the corner between the gymnasium and the slope Fru Haugen usually comes tripping down, her red hair on fire by the trees on the way to her music lessons. Arvid's leaning against the wall, smoking and looking at the flag-pole and the NLF colours flying. It is beautiful and unsettling at the same time; he smiles, a little cautiously, it seems, stubs out the cigarette and comes up to me. We are both late for different reasons, almost everyone has gone in for the first lesson and there are no teachers around. Together we walk to the hall with our bags over our shoulders.

'OK then,' I say, 'that's what you had to do?'

'Yes,' he says, 'and now I guess there will be trouble.'

'Did you expect anything else?'

'Hell, no.'

And trouble there is. We have history with Wollebæk. After half an hour Arvid and Bente have tangled him in a long debate about imperialism and India's development after Gandhi and then there is a knock at the door and in comes the headmaster. He reads out two names. They get to their feet and go with him. The two are Arvid and Henrik. When the bell rings they still haven't returned, but outside, on the steps, we see them standing by the flagpole arguing with the headmaster. He wants them to climb up the pole to bring down the flag. They refuse. Students come streaming out and stand around them in a circle. The yard is packed, the headmaster waving with his hands, he's warning them. Arvid and Henrik turn their back on him. Many Young Conservatives shout *Boo!* And the Young Socialists shout *Victory To The NLF!* but everyone else is just waiting to see what will happen. The headmaster turns to the crowd and starts to speak about 1814 and the founding fathers at Eidsvoll and the WAR and those who fought in it and what they would think if they saw foreign colours flying from a Norwegian flagpole. He waves his finger like a demagogue and stabs his points home, but his voice is unimpressive, it cracks on the high note, and those standing close to him, they grin and cover their mouths with their hands, and some at the back of the crowd jeer loudly, and Arvid turns and shouts:

'But goddamnit, there is a difference, isn't there! That flag,' he shouts, pointing to the top of the pole, 'is goddamnit the flag of an occupied country, just like we were! And the occupier is goddamnit the United States of America, that you're so happy to have bossing the Norwegian foreign policy through NATO!' The Young Conservatives howl as if possessed, they stamp their yachting shoes, jump up and down in their blue blazers and the headmaster's face goes blotchy. I am still standing on the steps looking over the heads in front of me, and what I see is Simen Bjørnsen, the head of the school's Young Conservatives, the Boy Scout, the great sportsman, on his way up the flagpole. He climbs like a monkey, he's a *natural*, and before anyone has really taken it in, he is halfway up. The schoolyard explodes, it's worse than on sports day, and as Simen slaps his hand on the top, unties the flag and lets it sail over the playground red and blue and yellow, and really, I don't give a damn about this. I guess it's all very important, but I am up to my neck in my own troubles, and it almost makes me throw up.

The crowd disperses and Arvid comes plodding after the headmaster towards his office. He looks defiant and lonely as he passes, and I pat him on the shoulder. He turns and looks into my eyes, but doesn't see there what he is looking for, for he doesn't even try to smile, just walks behind the headmaster with Henrik at his heels, and I don't see him again that day.

Neither do I see him the next day, and when I get home from school I give him a call, and his mother tells me he has been expelled for a week. Two days for the flag and three days for swearing at the headmaster. And also, his conduct grade has fallen a notch, and if he behaves like this again, they won't allow him to take his final exams. His father is in a rage, his mother tells me, though she seems quite unconcerned herself.

'Can I talk to him?'

'He's out walking.'

'Oh, is he. Where, then?'

'I have no idea. I guess it's me who should be asking you. Where do you two usually go?'

I know, of course, but I'm not telling her.

'Don't ask. I'll find him. Bye.'

I get dressed and go out and along the Sing-Sing balcony that runs along the third floor. What I really should have been doing is the afternoon round with *Aftenposten*, but I said I couldn't do it any more. It was too much, I didn't get my homework done. And, to tell the truth, I was fed up with it. At school I'm exhausted because I get up well before dawn, and so I sit there at my desk knowing I have to go out again as soon as I get home. It's one thing delivering papers before people get up in the morning, another being on display when everybody's outside doing whatever or sitting by the window, watching me with some hilarious remark up their sleeve.

I walk past the Metro station, up along Veitvetveien to Trondhjemsveien and through the underpass and then zigzag up between the blocks in Slettaløkka. At the top, before the forest, is the fenced-off area of the Nike missile battalion with the tall lookout tower and the big iron gate and the sentry box. Today, the gate is open, but there is no guard. That's fine with me, I didn't plan to sneak in anyway.

The path into the forest starts just beyond the football pitch that the soldiers and local people share, and to the right are the cracked-up foundations of an old smallholding owned by the Linderud estate. The house was still standing when I moved here. I remember grey smoke from the chimney, snowflakes melting on the roof and a face in the shadows behind the window. She must be dead now. Below is the horse field. It slopes sharply down and rises again to the edge of the forest. Inside it is a clearing, and inside the clearing is a huge rock. It's twenty metres long and ten metres wide and shaped like a fortress it's easy to defend against enemy attacks, and then there are hollows where you can hide if there's an invasion and several secret passages out if you need to escape. I just caught the last wars before I got too old for that kind of thing, but Arvid grew up among these rocks, and this is where he goes when he wants to be alone. I walk across the meadow, there is only one horse, it's brown with white socks, it's just a horse, nothing special. On my way up I see him on the top of the rock with a book in his hand and a cigarette between his lips. Even from a distance, I can see it clearly in the corner

31

of his mouth, and he takes it out and blows smoke above the book, and the smoke curls in the autumn air, and it seems odd, like something I have seen in a film, and he stands up and watches me as I walk across the field.

For a moment there, it's difficult to be the one who is approaching. I almost turn and go back. He stands quite still watching me. Someone is watching me, and I don't know what he expects. I feel like going back. This has never happened before. Not with Arvid. He is my friend, we have been friends for five years, since the first break on the first day at school in the autumn of 1965, and hardly a day has passed when we haven't talked, and now here he is, watching me approach, and I do not know who it is that he sees.

But it's only a moment, and then things fall back into place, he raises the hand holding the book and I wave back, and what I'm thinking is, I will always get by on my own.

'Hi,' I say.

'Hi.' He climbs down from the rock.

'It's damn cold.'

'Hell, yes,' he says, a bit uncertain, because, in fact, it isn't cold any more, but it was this morning, and nothing else occurs to me just then, and the only sound is the sound of the horse snorting in the field. It's restless and tosses its head and backs away. We can't see what it is it's afraid of, but now it is prancing on stiff legs and suddenly rears round and gallops towards where we are standing. It all happens so fast, it is sudden and violent and now the horse does look remarkable, for it is a thing of beauty, and even though there are many beautiful things in this world, it is always a strange feeling when you actually *see* them. And what we see is this animal with ears pinned back, its brown skin steaming and legs like shadows beneath its belly, and the hooves hammering the ground like a train over jointed tracks. I feel Arvid go stiff. I grab his shoulder and go stiff myself, although I have grown up among horses, and the instant before it hits us, I can see everything around me with brilliant clarity: the brilliant blue autumn sky, the yellow ridges, yes, every leaf up close and binocular-sharp in the limpid air. I suck the air down and howl WAAAHH! The horse turns in a flash and veers to the right and comes to a halt another twenty metres down the field, its flanks quivering, and then lowers its neck and snatches a mouthful of grass as though nothing has happened.

'Goddamnit,' Arvid says, 'that was something. Do you think it would have knocked us down?'

'What? No, I've never heard of anything like that. I don't know what spooked it, but I knew it would stop.'

'You screamed.'

'Because it was so damn beautiful.'

Arvid throws himself down on to the grass with his arms stretched wide and bursts into laughter, and I too have to laugh, because what was awkward between us has evaporated in the wake of the horse. I sit down on a boulder and roll myself a cigarette.

'How are you? Your mother said you got a week.'

'I don't know, really. It was lousy being expelled, but now I have time to read more.' He waves his book. 'Strong stuff. Do you know it?'

It's Jan Myrdal's *Confessions of a Disloyal European*, that has just been published by Pax. I know Jan Myrdal. Arvid has been taking the Metro to Oslo East every weekend to buy the Swedish paper *Aftonbladet* where Myrdal has a column, but this book I haven't seen.

'You can have it when I've finished.'

'I can buy it myself. I guess I have more money than you have. How's Henrik?'

'We planned it together, but of course I was the one who hoisted the flag, and that's what I told them, so it was me who got expelled. But listen to this,' he says, and reads:

'"In Ceylon I talk to a nice European tea planter.

'""So how many people live in this district?' I ask.

'""We are only four families,' he says.

'""That's not very many,' I say.

'""And twenty-five thousand Tamils, of course,' he says."'

'Shit, let me see.' He hands me the book, and I read the page, and the next; it's pure, concise writing about things that you walk around turning over in your mind. I have to have this book, there is something different here, open, bold. I give it back.

'Come along,' I say, climbing the rock to the highest point and Arvid comes with me. From where we stand, we can see past the fields to Rødtvet and Kaldbakken and a tiny slice of Trondhjemsveien where the footpath descends to the houses in Veitvet. I point.

'Do you know who I saw there yesterday morning?'

'How would I know?'

'My father.'

'Your father? Hell, isn't he dead?'

'Did I ever say that?'

He thought for a moment. 'No, I guess you haven't. As far as I remember, you haven't said a thing about him, ever. That's why I thought he was dead.'

'No. He isn't dead.'

'I see,' Arvid says. He looks bewildered, and looks down at Trondhjemsveien as if there was something he could find there.

So now I've said it. I shouldn't have, because then I may have to tell him more. Arvid is my friend, and now he looks at me, and my mind goes dim, and all around me it's getting dark, the forest is dark, it's late in the day and no longer possible to see in between the trees. It's all shadows. I turn my back, but that doesn't make it any better, a chill runs up my spine, and I can't stand still. I start to move down the rock, jumping from boulder to boulder as fast as I can, and Arvid is behind me.

'Hey, you, wait, for Christ's sake.'

But I don't.

4

There is a man dressed in black wandering the paths in the great forest. He walks day and night with a grey rucksack on his back. In the rucksack he has a pistol. Sometimes there is a metallic clink when it knocks against other things he carries with him. But no one hears. Only he is walking these paths. His pace is even, confident and not too fast, he has all the time in the world. He walks twenty kilometres a day, and when evening falls, he lights a fire close to water. The flames illuminate his weather-beaten face and when he bends down to throw more wood on the fire, the black fringe falls across his forehead. He lies down to sleep a few hours, and then, in the night, he walks another ten kilometres. His blue eyes sparkle in the dark, an owl sits blinking on a branch, and he never takes a wrong turn. He wears brown rubber boots, and he crosses streams and bogs when he has to, and he climbs the ridges. On the last ridge he halts and looks about him with a thin smile. From the top he can see a broad valley with terraced houses and high-rises and a big road leading north. He has arrived now. He drops his rucksack in the heather and sits down on a rock. He rolls a cigarette, there is a hiss as he lights up, both the sun and moon are out and he sits there watching for a long time. His hands are large and brown and rough, and there are deep furrows down both his cheeks. From his rucksack he pulls out a bottle and takes a long swig; he screws up his eyes, tightens the top and puts the green bottle back. There is a clink, and again he smiles. He finishes his cigarette and stubs it out on the rock where he is sitting. He gets up and without looking back, he walks into the forest until he finds a place that feels right. There, he rests the rucksack against a tree, takes an axe and starts to build a shelter. He is working on it all day. It is small, but it's waterproof and solid: he has done this many times before. As night falls, he takes out a primus stove, pumps paraffin into the burner head, lights a match and puts a frying pan on top. He tosses bacon in the pan and sits on a tree stump to wait. He has all the time in the world.

The alarm clock glows half-past one and I have no idea what woke me up, but now I cannot sleep. Outside, the rain is falling, even and solid as a wall, a shushing wall. The street lamps flicker as I lean against the windowsill and look out. The grey Sing-Sing houses out there have sunk into the ground, been washed away. Just this rain and the street lamps.

I have been dreaming. I am trembling, my forehead feels heavy and there is sand behind my eyelids. I am still drunk and cannot collect my thoughts. The only thing I remember is the dream and Arvid in the doorway. I am on my way out and he is about to tell me something important, his arms cut the air, but we have drunk too much, there is a rushing in my ears and I cannot hear what he is saying. There is a warm glow from inside the living room, he is alone, his sister and his parents have taken the night ferry to Denmark. They are going to a funeral. He stands dark against the light and is the best friend I have ever had and it doesn't matter that I cannot hear what he is saying.

In the room the air is stale and clammy. I open the window, and the October night seeps in, heavy, moist, you can almost touch it, and I stand in front of the open window wearing only my underpants and feel like screaming. The skin down my thighs and stomach feels tight, and I beat my hand on the sill until it hurts.

In the dark I grope for my sweater and a pair of trousers, pull them on and sit in the armchair I got from the old three-piece we used to have in the living room. I fumble my way and find the tobacco and matches on the table. I roll a smoke and light up. The match flares, and for a split second the room is illuminated, a little shock to the eye, and then it goes dark again; darker, even.

I sit smoking, hearing the drumming from outside, then I get up and go to my desk, switch on the lamp that only gives off a muted light, open a drawer and take out a battered copy of *Penthouse*. I have seen it before, many times, I am sick of it, and yet I leaf through it. There is a sequence with two girls. They are so naked their skin gleams and must be so soft to the touch, they are touching each other and it does look genuine. I know it's not, but I look anyway. I thumb through and the two girls touch each other more, slim hands on shiny skin, their mouths half open, eyes half open, and then they are all over each other, and I close my eyes and think about Fru Karlsen, the skin on her neck down to her shoulders and then further down, and I unbutton my trousers and touch myself, my right hand firmly round my dick. And while I'm doing this, I think how sad it is to be sitting alone in a room in the middle of the night like this, and my own thoughts distract me, and I have to concentrate, have to look at the magazine again and it takes longer than usual and afterwards the room is empty and there is a draught from the open window. I throw the *Penthouse* out into the rain and close the window with a bang. Then I go into the bathroom and wash.

Back in the room, I switch off the lamp and light the cigarette that's gone out in the ashtray. Now only the glow of the cigarette is visible and the faint square that is the window. When I feel I'm tired, I lie on the bed with my clothes on. I am almost asleep when I hear a sound I have not heard for years. I get out of bed and tiptoe across the floor, into the hall and over to the door of my mother's bedroom. Through a crack in the doorway I can see the white back of a man moving. I do not know him, and I quickly turn round. He must have been in the house the whole time as there was no one up when I returned from Arvid's. This time I undress and lie close to the wall with the duvet tight around me.

I wake up and the sun is shining straight into my face. Someone has been in here and opened the curtains. I get out of bed, feel my head hurting a bit, but everything in the room is bright, and it's a bright blue morning, Sunday morning, and of course I can't remember my plan for the day. I roll a cigarette although it's stupid to smoke before breakfast, but I don't want to go downstairs yet. I watch the blue smoke curl under the ceiling, look at myself in the mirror above the dressing table, put my old sunglasses on and keep them on while I look at myself smoking. I hear the church bells chime from the top of the shopping centre.

I take a book from the shelf over my desk. It is worn, dog-eared with stains on the jacket, and then I get into bed and start reading. It was Arvid's father who said we ought to read that book, but Arvid had already read it, he has read all the books that are worth a damn, and his father must have known that. He only said it so he could add:

'Read this one, boys, then perhaps you'll understand what it's like to toil and sweat for the things you want!' Arvid groaned, but I read the book, and this is the third time now. It is called *Martin Eden* and was written by Jack London. I had read *The Call of the Wild* and *The Sea Wolf*, almost everyone we know has read them, but only Arvid and I have read *Martin Eden,* and we keep it to ourselves.

There is something about this book, and there is something about his struggle, and as soon as I had read it I knew I wanted to be a writer, and if I didn't make it, I would be an unhappy person.

I hear them talking down in the kitchen. There is a smell of fried bacon and coffee, but I don't want to go downstairs, and now that I have heard them, I find it difficult to concentrate on the book. I put it down and go over to the weights bench, which I have placed between the bed and the chest of drawers, lie down flat on my back and raise the bar from the stand and quickly pump it twenty times. I get up and add ten kilos on each side and do twenty more. I feel warm now, it's really too early in the day, but I don't care. I am really eager, and I double the weights, do quick, rhythmic lifts and feel my chest tighten, and my biceps, and my stomach is working like it should, going smooth and easy as a ball bearing. I know who I am, I am drenched and this is my sweat. Only my mother and I live here now, and that suits me fine.

I shower, splash and make a lot of noise, and as I turn the water off I hear the front door slam. I'm in no hurry, and when I come downstairs to the kitchen, she is alone, standing by the stove, looking out of the window with her mind somewhere else. I sit down at the table and look at her. She is forty-three years old. Then she turns and looks at me.

'When did *you* get home last night?' she says. Not a word about the man who has just left.

'I don't know, twelve, maybe half-past. I don't know. Anyway, you weren't up.'

'No, I wasn't.'

'Of course you weren't.'

She blushes, but refuses to say anything about the man who has left. 'You were at Arvid's, weren't you?' I nod and help myself to what's left of the bacon and a slice of bread.

'Isn't he supposed to be in Denmark? I heard his grandfather had died.'

'He didn't want to go there. I guess that's his business.'

My mother shrugs, I eat and then the telephone rings. We have a telephone now. She answers it cautiously. 'Hello?' she says.

'It's Arvid,' she says. I get up from the table, still chewing, and take the receiver.

'Hi,' I say, and chew a little slower for it is hard to make out what he's saying, but I understand that he wants me to come over. 'OK, I'll be right there,' I say and gently put the receiver down, and as I am doing so, I hear his voice again and I lift it quickly, but then it's the dialling tone.

'I have to rush,' I tell my mother and grab another piece of bread and eat it going into the hall and put my jacket on and my shoes.

'Didn't you say you would stay home today?'

'I never said that,' I say, and know full well I said so yesterday. I open the door and turn, and she is standing in the light from the kitchen window and is no more than a silhouette and that makes it easier.

'What about letting me know if more than the two of us will be living here?' I say, and I am outside before she has the time to answer.

5

I walk up Beverveien towards the Metro station by the shopping centre. It is twelve o'clock. Over the rooftops I can hear the bells ringing after church. It's still cold, but the sky is all blue and the sun is thawing the mud on the road, and it leaves grey-brown stripes on my shoes, and outside the station there are shards of glass and blood-stains on the tarmac. They are pink and pale after the night. On the corner in front of Stallen, which used to be Glasmagasinet, people are looking at the display they have seen a hundred times before. They're pretending to be out for a Sunday stroll. But I know them and know they are circling the centre waiting for Geir's bar to open at one. They just can't stay at home any longer and keep their fists in their pockets to hide their shaking hands. I feel like yelling at them, for Christ's sake pull yourselves together, and stay out of my way! I know they won't pull themselves together, it's too late. They are old, their days are over, everything they have known is gone, all the things they could do, and now here they stand, scraping their feet against the ground, letting the clock tick them closer to their first gulp, and then they'll sit and drink until their bodies calm down and will talk rubbish about everything being so wonderful, and when evening comes, they have to go home, and so they fall asleep early and hope their dreams won't be too bad, and then they wake up the next morning as always.

I open my jacket at the neck, I suck in the air and expand my chest to its limit, and then I walk round to the lower side of the shopping centre and along Grevlingveien to Veitvetsvingen and down to the house where Arvid lives.

I knock first, and then I ring the bell, but there is no answer even though I wait for about five minutes, so I turn the handle, and the door is open, and I step into the hall.

'Arvid?' I call, not too loud, and there is no response. I walk on into the living room and see that he has thrown up in the middle of the floor. Luckily for him there is lino down and not the wall-to-wall carpet almost everyone has now. I go into the kitchen and fill a bucket of water, find a rag and wash the floor and pour the crap down the sink and flush it with hot water so it will all go away. That's no easy job. What's left I have to remove with a paper towel and throw in the waste bin. I take the bin bag from the stand, tie it up and put it in the hall ready to be carried out. The smell is not the greatest, so I open the door.

I wash my hands and go back to the living room and head for the stairs. At the foot of the stairs there is a bookcase with Tolstoy and Ingstad and Gorky and Jack London and all the others. It belongs to Arvid's father, from before the war, but Arvid took it over long ago. It has rose carvings along the front at the top and women's bodies and men's faces down the sides, and the wood is dark with oil and not like anything else in the flat. I run my fingers over one of the female bodies, then go upstairs, the steps creaking as they always do, and I can hear Arvid groan inside his room.

I look in and there he is, lying flat on the bed with his clothes on and his head over the edge, talking into a bucket.

'Interesting conversation,' I say, and walk straight in and open the window because the air is thick and bad for his health.

'Comedian,' he gurgles into the bucket. On the floor is the ashtray we used last night, full of dog ends. I pick it up, empty the mess down the toilet and wash it in the sink. The bottle beside the bed was half full when I left last night. It's empty now.

'Have you heard the news on the radio?' I ask.

'No, Goddamnit.'

'Nixon's announced a full withdrawal.'

'What!?' He yanks his head up from the bucket. 'Is that true?'

'No, but you could do with a shower. It's not beyond you.'

'Idiot!' He tries to stand up, and his face goes all white and he has to sit back down. He swallows and struggles with something stuck in his throat.

'Come on,' I say, but he is resting his head on his arms and looks as if maybe he's crying. I go out and find a towel in the cupboard by the bathroom and toss it through the door. It hits him on the forehead.

'Pull yourself together. Get into that shower, and then we're out of here.' I go downstairs and sit down in the living room and roll a cigarette. At first it is quiet up there, and then I hear him shuffling across the floor, and at last the shower starts, a trickle at first and then stronger, and I go to the balcony door and stand in the sun, smoking. It's nice and warm against the sunny wall, and I close my eyes and finish the cigarette and flick the butt on to the lawn. Back in the living room, I go to the bookcase, run my fingers over the spines and stop at the centenary editions of Tolstoy from 1928 and wonder if Arvid's father has really read them all. I pull out the first volume of *Anna Karenina*, read the first sentence I have read many times before:

'All happy families resemble each other; each unhappy family is unhappy in its own way,' it says, and Arvid turns off the shower. I put the book on the shelf and slump into a chair and wait. It takes him ten minutes to come down, still pale, but he is clinging on.

'Mush, mush!' he says, as Helge Ingstad does in his book *Trapper's Life* when he wants the dogs to set off. It's been our code for years and seems a bit childish now, but I take the hint and jump to my feet and say:

'Did you ask about the car?'

'I had to sweet-talk him for half an hour,' he says and pulls the keys from his pocket.

'Will you drive or shall I?'

'Are you out of your mind? I'm not sober.' He throws me the keys and I catch them with one hand, grab my jacket from the chair and walk towards the door.

'Don't forget the bin bag on your way out,' I say.

We take Trondhjemsveien out of town to Gjelleråsen Ridge. The car is a black Opel Kadett, not exactly the latest model, but well looked after, and I feel good sitting behind the wheel. I have had my licence for two months; Arvid and I took our tests at the same time. Before that, I had only driven a tractor out in the countryside. The cars were Egil's thing, he was obsessed and pestered his way into most of those around our place from the time he was ten, but I do like the movement and freedom and always stretch the speed limit. Arvid rolls his window down all the way, and his head is almost out of the car, the wind blows in and it gets cold, but he shuts his eyes and opens his mouth and refuses to roll the window back up.

'You'll get your head chopped off or a sparrow down your throat,' I say.

'Aw, shut up,' he answers and I swerve the car wheel to give him a scare, but he doesn't care.

'Leaving Oslo,' I say as we pass the sign by Skillebekk. 'Akershus County next. Nittedal or Skedsmo?'

'Skedsmo,' he says from outside the car, and I turn at the crossroads at the top of the ridge and drive down the long, winding hill behind Mortens Kro, the restaurant there, and on to the Hellerud plain.

'Please, not Lillestrøm.'

'OK.' I turn into the road for Nittedal church and Solberg, down a steep incline and cross the narrow bridge over the Nitelva river. Along the banks there are boys with fishing rods casting their lines and having a good time in the warming sun. One of them has just landed a perch, its scales glinting, and I stop the car and watch. Arvid opens the door, gets out and goes over to a bush where he throws up and then slides down the embankment to the river and washes his face in the ice cold water.

'We should have brought fishing tackle,' he says, coming

back up behind the car and is in a cheery mood all of a sudden.

'Well it's too late now, you have soiled the water.'

He gets back in, and I do a perfect hill start without the handbrake. The fields rise steeply on both sides of the river and yellow and grey they arch in a pattern of shapes and lines against the blue sky, and I don't know why, but it *does* something to me.

'Left or right?' I ask at the first junction.

'Right, or else we'll be back in Nittedal.' I turn right, up a gravel road and wonder what's with him and Nittedal.

The road winds between sloping fields and slowly climbs, and then we are at the top. Down to the left, the valley opens beneath a lattice of shadows and light on the meadow, and moving north it narrows into a funnel and only the gleaming road heads on to Harestua. We can barely make out Glitre Sanatorium, its solid yellow shape in the foothills. There is a strong wind here: a gust catches the car and almost blows us into the ditch, and I wrench the wheel against the wind and the car lurches forward like a drunk man's car, and I give Arvid a glance and wonder how his gut feels. But he laughs, he's having a good time.

'Step on it,' he says, leaning back and putting his feet on the dashboard. 'Shit, I feel so much better now.'

We enter Skedsmo by Nittedal church through a grove of spruce trees. There are a few houses, and there is a bus shelter, and Arvid points at the trees.

'Do you remember when we trudged through those trees to the Krakoseter cabins with our rucksacks down round our knees? We had to sing the Scout song the whole way.

Do you remember when you got your pants filled with Coke? Being a Scout was such great fun.'

I do remember, and I remember exactly how much fun the Scouts were. We had joined the Scouts for a year because of the trips they went on, and I remember that one time I didn't finish a cross-country run because I'd been lying in the heather watching a fox attack a pigeon. The Scout leaders came crashing and yelling through the forest and scared the fox out of its wits and dragged me down to the cabins. And when we were there, I had to stand on my hands out in the yard surrounded by Girl Guides while two leaders held me up by the feet and a third poured a bottle of Coke down each trouser leg. Then they forced me to walk around for two hours without changing my clothes while the Coke dried into sticky patches all over my body. When at last they allowed me to wash and I had borrowed some clean clothes from Arvid, I went into the leaders' room and punched the scout-master. He was even a member of the goddamn Rotary Club.

I remember the burnt bread over the fire and the burnt sausages and the assistant Scout leader who was thirty-five and still lived with his mother and always wanted to ask the new boys back to his room at home. We're going to a jamboree in America in the autumn and have to discuss it, he kept saying, and who didn't want to go to America? But he was the only person who had ever heard about that trip to America, and I remember how relieved I was when I walked alone down the path through the forest to the bus stop on my last day after being expelled from the Scouts, and I promised myself I would never join anything organised again.

'You still remember it, don't you?' Arvid asks and starts singing, and I chime in and soon we bawl at the top of our voices:

Dear father in heaven so high, hear my heart's silent prayer, toiling on earth beneath the sky, give me the strength and wit to care, help me to live by thine own son's creed, to honour my parents, the land and laws, and help all others in word and deed, obeying Scout vows and aiding our cause!

And we remember every word and every note of the song, and know we will never forget them for as long as we live.

At the Skedsmo junction the road goes north to Gjerdrum. There are fields on both sides the whole way, and behind them is the dense forest. The road twists and turns, goes up hill and down dale, and the driving is never boring. I keep the speed up as much as I dare, go even faster on the straights and change down before the bends and try to stay as close as possible to the point when the Opel just might lose traction and skid off the road, but not quite, because the car is not mine. The telephone poles flash past, and I feel a rush in my body that is new and makes my head spin, and now would be a good time to hear Jimi Hendrix play 'Crosstown Traffic' or 'Purple Haze'. Arvid sits quietly with his hair blown back, just watching, then he picks up his tobacco and rolls two cigarettes, lights them both with the dashboard lighter and pokes one in my mouth.

'God, it's wonderful,' he says. 'I've never been here before. Is this where you come from?'

'Not quite.'

Not quite, but not far off either. I thought I had forgotten how everything looked, but I haven't forgotten a thing.

I have not forgotten the cornfields in autumn, or Lake Aurtjern in July or the apple tree outside my window, and all I had to do was reach out and pick an apple, or the long gravel road where Siri Skirt used to walk and show her bottom for two ten øre coins, and she wasn't wearing anything underneath, and once I was allowed to walk round twice while she held her skirt up under her chin; or the rafting holiday on Lake Hurdal. My father forced me to come with him, and made me pull up a pike that scared me witless, and when I refused, he hit me in the face, and then I hammered a nail into my foot, and we were forced to go home.

'Hey, look at the petrol gauge,' Arvid suddenly shouts, 'we're out of petrol. Have you got any money? I think I'm skint.' He puts his hand in his pocket and we pull into the Shell station in Ask and empty our pockets. We have twenty-five kroner between us. I let the car roll to the first petrol pump and sit waiting for Arvid to get out and fill up. But he doesn't move. We stare straight ahead, and we don't speak, and then he says:

'I've never filled a car with petrol.'

'Me neither.'

'I don't even know where the petrol tank is. Do you?'

'I have no idea.'

'Perhaps they come out and do it for us?'

'They stopped doing that ages ago.'

'Shit.'

We both get out and walk round the car and realise we have parked on the wrong side of the pump. Then a Ford Granada drives in, and a man in a hat and coat jumps out, and his face is flushed. He yanks the nozzle from the pump, bangs the cap open and stuffs the nozzle in and then he gawps at the pump, his lips moving, mumbling words I can't make out, and then I see that what he is gawping at is the kroner counter, and what he is mumbling is the numbers as they tick by. He is at it for a long time, and we pretend we are discussing our route, and at the same time we are studying every move he makes. When he goes in to pay I hurry to the Opel and back it into position and do what he did before I forget, and hope it's the right kind of petrol. I put in twenty-five kroners' worth. Then I enter the kiosk with an unlit cigarette in my mouth trying to look as if it's something I do every day.

After a few more kilometres heading north, I turn off the main road on to a bumpy gravel track. It rounds a sharp bend, and stones and ruts on the road pound the wheels and make everything shake. Then the road plunges down, and at the bottom of the hill there is a bridge over the river Leira where the rapids start. In the woods on the other side I glance in between the trees to see if my shack is still standing. It is not.

'Fancy going for a visit?'

'A farmer?'

'A kind of farmer, yes. He lives right over there. Leif is his name. If he isn't dead.'

'OK, but if he's dead I don't want to see him.'

'You were funnier with a hangover.'

I stop and change down to first and climb the hills on the other side of the river. We pass a few model farms, painted red and white the way they're supposed to be, rose beds and everything neat and tidy, and Arvid looks around, his eyes full of expectation. He hasn't a clue where we're going. A few minutes later I see Tommy's barn at the top of a steep slope. There is not a level square metre of land on his property. Some goats are grazing on the slope. At one time the barn was yellow, and he was so proud that this was the only yellow barn in the district, but now the paint is peeling and it is more grey than yellow. The odd board has gone missing, and we can see straight into the hayloft. There isn't much hay. Behind the barn, you can see the farmhouse with its sway-backed roof, and once it was white, but now it is as grey as the barn. It is only five years ago, it must have looked the same then, but it did not *seem* like it.

We have to drive on a bit to find the driveway, and I keep looking for the blue letterbox that used to be a land-mark before, but the box has fallen off and is lying on the ground, and I have to back up the car. I turn into the driveway and pick up speed, and as I remember it, there was a pothole in the road so muddy after rains that you had to have a tractor pull you out if you got stuck, and it probably isn't any better now. And it isn't. I put my foot down and shoot across, the mud flying everywhere. The rear of the Opel bounces into the air and Arvid jumps around in his seat and shouts:

'Hey, take it easy, for fuck's sake. This is my dad's car! He'll kill me!' But I am driving fast now, because I have second thoughts and wonder how I got myself into this. But it's too late to turn back, and I want this over and done with.

There are three cars in the yard. Not one of them has four wheels. They have stood there for a good while and one of them I remember very well. It's an old Volvo station wagon that was used for everything from transporting piglets to delivering the dead on commission, and these were the only times the car was washed. The other two are what Egil called 'crash cars'. You buy them as wrecks, get the engine running and drive them until they fall apart and leave them wherever they break down. A chicken cackles and sticks its head out of a smashed window. From where I am standing, I see nothing that can move under its own steam: even the wheelchair by the farmhouse door is missing a wheel and is lying on its back, rusting where someone left it.

A man in stained overalls comes round the corner of the barn and stands squinting, shading his eyes from the sun.

'Hi, Bjørn,' I say, and he shakes his head and strokes his jaw. Then he scuttles into a shed without saying or doing anything.

'Who was that?' Arvid asks.

'Bjørn. Farm boy.'

'Farm *boy*? He must be at least seventy.'

I scratch my head. 'About seventy-two.'

'Is he always so talkative?'

'Bjørn never says a word.' I walk over to the house and

knock at the door. No one answers, so I push it and go in through porch and call through the open kitchen door:

'Hello, anyone at home?' I hear a shuffle of feet and a woman of about thirty I have never seen before comes from the kitchen and looks surprised. There is something wrong with her legs. She doesn't lift them when she walks.

'Does Leif still live here?'

'He sure does.'

'My name's Audun Sletten. I spent a summer here a few years back and I thought I would come by and say hello.'

'Well, I don't know, he's asleep.'

Fine, I think, we'll be out of here, but then I hear his voice from the living room.

'Who is it, Ingrid?'

'Young man called Audun. He's come by, he says.'

'Audun? Is that Audun, you say? I'll be damned, be right there.' There is a bit of a commotion, he groans as if he is making a serious effort, and then comes wheeling into the kitchen. He looks exactly as he used to, the grey crew-cut hair, his sculpted face like some bust I have seen in a magazine, and his upper body like a chunk of rock. But his legs are thinner, they don't seem to carry him any more. There was some trouble with his legs before, but I didn't see the wheelchair coming. I go up to him and shake his hand and he holds mine in both of his.

'Well, if it ain't Audun. It's been a while.'

'Summer of '65.'

'And now it's 1970, that makes it more than five years. I'll be damned, you're big now. And strong too, I can see that. You've got a friend with you, a long-haired baboon?'

55

He laughs without malice, Arvid grins and goes to shake hands.

'Arvid Jansen. I look after Audun.'

'Oh, so he still needs that, does he? Well, I guess we too did that for a while, back then. I'm only joking. Audun was a boy who could look after himself. Be wrong to say anything else. He came here with that white bum of his, and welcome he was, that's for sure. He could graft like an adult even though he was no more than a half-pint.'

'White bum?' Arvid whispers.

'Shh,' I say. 'And Signe, is she here?'

Leif takes a deep breath and says:

'I guess she moved. Lives somewhere in Trøndelag I've heard, I'm not really sure.' He smacks his hands on the wheelchair. 'And here I sit. But it's fine, it's fine. Ingrid helps me indoors and Bjørn outdoors. It's fine.'

But I don't see how it can be fine out here, or going anywhere but down the drain. Something must have happened, and I cannot ask. Signe with the large bosom and her large smile, Signe with her soft hands on her way up to the first floor where I was lying in bed that last summer, full of yellow fever and not able to sleep. Their children had moved out a long time ago, so the whole room was mine. Her white shift in the grey from the skylight, Signe with her white gentle words, Signe so kind. But I cannot ask. Once I sent a card, but there was no answer.

'You see, somehow she fell ill. Well, let's not talk about that now. Jesus, it's nice to see you again, Audun. How's your mother getting on down there?'

'A lot better,' I say. 'A heck of a lot better.'

He looks at me with those fiercely blue eyes. 'Yes, I guess she is.' He strokes his chin and his bristles rasp loud enough for all of us to hear. He clears his throat takes another deep breath and says:

'You know, your father was here a month ago. Strange you should come now. He was out of here, he said. He left his accordion, it was too heavy to carry with him. He said he was going far. I could just keep it, he didn't give a shit, if you'll pardon the expression. There it is.' He points to a corner of the large kitchen. All the junk is still there, I remember a lot of it, and straight away I recognise the worn, brown case. I go over and open the case and there it is, black and white with red stripes on the bellows, a Paolo Soprani. I bend down and run my fingers across the keys as if the notes might come, but they don't. For people with thick blood, I think. I look up at Leif. He is looking at me.

'He didn't look too friendly when he left, Audun, I have to say. But I don't know what to do with that squeezebox. None of us here can play. Perhaps you could take it with you? That would be good. Then it would stay in the family, like.'

He crossed the line there speaking of family, and he knows it, so I don't answer. I look down at the accordion.

'Fine,' I say, 'we'll take it with us,' and Arvid, who has heard about this accordion, is about to speak, but then he catches himself before the words come out. The air in the kitchen goes quiet, and we stand there hardly daring to breathe. I think fast and say:

'What happened to Toughie, the fox you kept on a chain behind the barn?'

'Oh him,' Leif says and tells the story of the fox that thought he was a dog and was kept on a rope behind the barn, and the hens refused to sit on their eggs as long as he was there. But everybody loved that fox and didn't want to let him go, so Leif had to brood the eggs in his armpits and in the end Signe, Bjørn and all the guests were walking around with eggs in their armpits until they had aches and pains all over. Dinner was especially difficult, Leif says, and demonstrates how they had to sit at the table with their arms down by their sides, all posh like, and hold their knives and forks like aristocrats.

'In the end we had better manners than the Sun King,' Leif says, and Arvid laughs, and Ingrid hums by her bench, and as we leave I grab the case by the handle and promise to be back soon now that I have my driver's licence.

We put the accordion on the rear seat and drive out of the yard. After the pool of mud Arvid says:

'Why did you take the accordion?'

'I don't know.'

'You can't even play it.'

'I'm telling you, I don't know.'

'I don't think your mother will be too happy about it, now that you know he's close by. Do you believe in fate now or what?'

'For fuck's sake, I don't know, I keep telling you! Goddamnit, why can't you leave me in peace!' I come out of the drive and turn too sharply round the bend and hit a fence post and it scrapes against the door, and I jump on the brakes. We both sit there. Arvid's face is white.

'Oh shit, I'm sorry,' I say.

'It was *my* fault. I should've kept my mouth shut.'

We open the doors. Leif's house is on the opposite side of a hollow, but if anyone is standing in the window, I can't see them. The car door is not as bad as I thought, but there is quite a scratch in the paintwork. But no dent. Arvid runs his hand along the door.

'It won't be cheap. The whole door will have to be resprayed.'

'I can pay. I'm going to stop anyway,' I say.

'Stop what?'

'Stop school.'

'That's the stupidest thing I've ever heard. You've got less than a year left. Weren't you going to be a writer?'

'You won't be a writer just because you finish school. Did Jack London finish school? Did Gorky? Or Lo-Johansson or Nexø, or Sandemose, or anyone else worth reading?'

'For Christ's sake, Audun, that was a hundred years ago! No one went to school for long then! Today everybody does!'

'Not me. I'm going to get a job.'

Arvid sits down in the ditch and starts throwing stones into the field, small ones at first and then bigger and bigger and he gets up and finds himself a big piece of rock and heaves it with both hands as far and as hard as he can and he yells:

'Goddamnit!' He turns. 'What's happening here?' he says.

'Nothing. I'll just quit school.'

'It's not only that,' he says, 'and you know it.'

6

Egil was two years younger than me, and I am pretty certain I can remember when he was born. Or maybe I am mixing it up with stories Kari has told me.

One story goes like this.

Kari and I are alone at home. She is six and is supposed to be looking after me. My mother and father are away. *She* is at Stensby hospital having Egil, but I don't understand that, only that both of them are away and Kari is with me, and anyway this is not the first time. It's funny the things you don't forget. There is a knock on the living-room window and I turn and see my father's face through the glass. He looks strange. He is waving one hand and making faces, and his face fills the window. The door is locked, and he has lost his key. Kari goes to open it. She doesn't really want to. I hear a bang and run into the hall and see my father lying face down on the floor. He is laughing into the floorboards. I hurry over and sit on his back, but then he gets up and I fall off, hitting my shoulder on the shoe rack. It hurts. I scream, but he doesn't care. He goes over to the cupboard in the living room, it is called grandfather's cabinet, I already know that. He bursts into laughter and says:

'Now there are three of you. We have to celebrate.' I don't understand what he means, but he takes the pistol from the cupboard. I must have seen it before. It has been one object among many; now it is different. He lifts his arm and fires three shots into the ceiling. We cover our ears, the loud cracks make our bodies shake.

'I'll never forget it,' Kari says. 'I thought my head would explode.' We have been to the Grorud Cemetery and are walking along Trondhjemsveien on our way home. My mother is a few steps behind us, she's crying and wants to be left alone. It's Egil's sixteenth birthday. It's a Friday in October. I have taken the day off from school, and when we get home, Jussi Björling will be on the turntable. She always plays opera when something is wrong, she plays opera when nothing is wrong, she always plays opera no matter what. Sometimes she locks the door, turns the volume up and stands on a chair conducting with her eyes closed. I have seen her through the window on my way from friends' houses at Linderud, I have looked across the little hollow with the stream and into our apartment on the third floor and seen how my mother is standing on a chair conducting the music I cannot hear, and wondered how many other people have seen her.

And almost always it is Jussi Björling. There is a signed photograph of him on the living-room wall. How she got hold of that, no one knows, but it has always seemed impressive, has given her records some extra meaning, and it was on the wall of our house in the country. My father couldn't stand it, he did not like opera, he liked tango and anything else was for people with thin blood. On his own accordion he could play the tango, and people said he was pretty good.

'Jussi Björling? Hell, he looks like a pen pusher!' he used to say, and once, when he was in a drunken haze, he smashed some of her records.

'We were lucky the neighbours called the police,' Kari says. 'Things could have got out of hand. You were only two years old, for Christ's sake. He was so drunk. He was always so goddamn drunk. Was I happy when we moved at last.'

We talk about him as though he, too, were dead, we do that every time we talk about him. It's not often. But he isn't dead.

We walk down Trondhjemsveien. Flaen and Kaldbakken are on the lower side where many from my class live. Among them is Venke. I know exactly which window is hers. I have been there with her, kissing on her bed with my hand up her skirt and her hand down my pants, and with her mouth against my neck she whispered: 'I think maybe I love you, you're so strong.' That really scared me, so I took off.

These houses seemed so important before, but now they look like something from a cartoon, compared with the high-rises at Ammerud. Rødtvet is on the upper side, and behind it is forest and more forest, for hours and days if that's what you want. You can go in there and keep wandering and come out again far into the countryside.

'It took him five years to get here,' I say. 'He must have fallen asleep on the way.'

'What are you talking about?'

'He's here now. I saw him just over a week ago, at the end of my paper round.'

'Who's here now?'

'The person we're talking about. Dad.'

What a word! Dad. But there is no other.

'He was standing there, at the top of that hill.' I point to where the footpath slopes down from Trondhjemsveien, by the Metro bridge. 'The man in the black suit. The man with the shiny pistol. I wonder if he still has it. Perhaps it's in his rucksack. And it was definitely his rucksack.'

'You must be kidding! Are you sure?' Kari grabs my arm and walks a bit faster to leave our mother further behind.

'Of course I'm sure. Do you think I have forgotten what he looks like?'

'Have you told her?' Kari tries not to turn round, but doesn't quite succeed.

'What would be the point of that? I don't want to move again. Not now, at least. I'm not scared of him.'

'Oh no?' She looks at me, and I know as well as her that I am scared to death. He is the only person who really scares me. Everything else is child's play.

'I'll kill him,' I say.

'Shh, don't talk like that. But what does he want? What do you think he wants? We'll have to work out something. It's too bad I have to go home on the bus tonight.'

'To your car spray hotshot?'

She blushes. 'You mind your own business!'

'There's nothing to work out. We'll just have to wait and see what happens.'

We stop until my mother has caught up with us so we can walk together down Grevlingveien. She is not crying any more, and Kari slips her arm under hers, and she smiles at us.

My mother is small and fair-haired, quite slim, and if you are not standing too close and can't see the lines around her eyes and mouth, thirty-six is not the first age that springs to mind. I suppose you could say she is attractive, I don't know, it's hard for me to say. Once, around where we used to live, I saw her turn a man's head on the road, but maybe she had smudged her lipstick or had a black eye that day. She had one from time to time. So did I. When my father was home for long enough, we all did.

She has always wanted curly hair, but it is straight as a waterfall, just like mine, and it seems to me that fair-haired people are not as curly as dark-haired people. Anyway, she has tried curlers and tongs and once she saved up to have a perm. When she came home she stood crying in front of the mirror because the curls were compact and tight and not what she had pictured and dreamt about, and, to be frank, she did look terrible. For almost an hour she stood over the basin trying to smooth her hair out again, and she stayed indoors for several days. So much money down the drain. What she does now is fill the kettle, put it on the stove, and when the water boils she hangs her hair over the gushing steam, and then the tips curl and give her what she calls a natural wave.

Since we moved, she has really had only one good friend. His name is Robert, but he calls himself Roberto, and he rented our spare bedroom the first difficult year in Veitvet. Now he lives in a smart one-room flat in Majorstua on the west side. He drives a white MGB, digs opera and is a homo. That doesn't seem to bother him much, and it doesn't bother me either. Sometimes he pinches my bum, but that's just teasing, to show he knows that I know that he isn't *actually* pinching my bum. Or something like that.

Every Wednesday afternoon Roberto drives to Veitvet from Majorstua to listen to opera with my mother. The white car floats down Beverveien with the roof rolled back, round the curve, and Roberto waves his hand to the boys standing along the road and the boys wave back, and it doesn't seem to bother anyone that he is a homo. But I may be wrong there.

As we go up the steps in the tower and along the Sing-Sing gallery he is standing outside our door with a bouquet of flowers and a plastic bag in his hand, even though it's only two days since he was last here, and I think that maybe homos have a feel for that kind of thing, like girls do. Anyway, my mother smiles and pulls herself together and is happy. Now there is someone to share the opera with, and I'm happy too, because I don't have to stay at home and be a comfort. Some days it makes me feel claustrophobic and today is one of them.

I go up to my room and change into normal clothes, hold up my checked trousers before I go for the Wranglers instead. Before I leave, I play Bob Dylan's 'Like a Rolling Stone' to cleanse my mind. It's unbeatable. It is so full of hatred it makes me want to lie down on the bench and pump iron, but it will take too long. I can't be indoors now, not with Kirsten Flagstad and Maria Callas howling in the next room.

On my way out, I hit my foot against something sticking out from under the bed. It's the accordion. I sneaked it indoors and up to my room when my mother wasn't there and have hidden it. I have a KEEP OUT sign on my door to make her stay away. I haven't mentioned it to anyone, only Arvid knows, and sometimes I feel an urge to take it out, hold it in my arms and play a few notes. But I am afraid it will make me remember too much. I push it back underneath with my foot.

I walk through the living room. Roberto is standing by the old record cabinet waving a new recording of Tosca, and he winks at me, and I pat my bum, and my mother says, 'Well, put it on, then.'

The first notes come thundering down the stairs as I leave the building. She plays music louder than I do, and yet I am the one who gets a hard time. I guess I appreciate Jussi Björling more than she does Jimi Hendrix. The only singer for her after 1945 is Elvis. I couldn't give a shit about him. But maybe Elvis reminds her of the days when the future was still open and she sat around in old American cars necking with my father, dreaming behind the dashboard with Kari in the back seat wrapped in nappies, and was about to marry this man that she wanted. What a kick in the teeth.

It's raining outside. Heavy, gusting rain, and the concrete walls of the houses turn sticky and dark. It makes me feel so out of place, and suddenly I long for thatched houses and log walls and attics and birch trees right outside your window and meadowland where the wind and the rain sweep across the tall grass in one long, surging swell and make you think of films you have seen and of walking barefoot, and then it painfully passes and is squeezed into a funnel with only one narrow way out.

There is nothing to work out. We just have to wait and see what happens. But nothing happens. Soon two weeks have gone, and had I not been the person I am, I would have thought it was a ghost I had seen. I remember a time out in the country when almost everyone believed in ghosts. Someone had planted stories that spread all over the district like a nervous disease, and in the end Kari was so scared she joined something called Kløfta Parapsychological Association. Its members went off in droves to old abandoned farms and lay on the living room floors with tape recorders, keeping each other awake, rigid with fear, waiting for white ladies in lace frocks. But girls are girls, and what I believe is what I see when I see it. I have never seen any ghosts. The ones that haunt me do not glide around at night wearing lace frocks, howling with grief.

Perhaps I had got it wrong. But I had *not*, and then there is the accordion and what Leif said, although I don't understand just why he went to Leif. Anyway, it *was* him. But what does he want? What is he waiting for?

I walk along Beverveien in the rain, turn up the collar of my reefer jacket and feel the rain running off my hair down my neck, and the sun breaks through, and even though it's very low, it feels like spring, only colder. I could go into the woods now, take the paths from the top of Slettaløkka into the forest and on to Lake Alunsjøen and down around Lake Breisjøen to Ammerud. I often do that, it's a fine route if you walk fast. I like walking fast. But that road is closed to me now.

Arvid is standing outside the Narvesen kiosk by the Metro station buying cigarettes. He has just got off the train after school and is still carrying his schoolbag. I lean against one of the columns under the bridge and wait until he has finished. After the long drive into the country, I have only seen him at school. We have barely spoken, which is quite unusual, and he smiles in a shy way as he turns and sees me standing there.

'Hi,' he says. 'You weren't at school today. Have you stopped coming?'

'We were at the cemetery.'

He nods, and then I ask:

'How did it go with the car door?'

'Dad got all worked up, of course. But now it's all sprayed and done.'

'How much was it?'

'A hundred kroner. But don't worry. I said it was my fault, so Dad paid.'

'No way. It was my fault.' I pull my wallet out and take a hundred-kroner note. I've just been paid for the paper round. My mother will have to wait for her share. 'Here,' I say.

'Bloody hell, Audun, you know you don't have to pay.'

'What's right is right, or else everything would just be crap. Take the money, I'll be all right, no problem.' He takes the note folds it and puts it in his pocket.

'So, you're not quitting school then?'

'That's a whole other thing. Coming?'

'Where to?'

'Well, not the woods, that's for sure. To town maybe, or Geir's?'

'Geir's? I thought you hated the place.'

'It's early. None of the jokers are there yet. I feel like a beer. It has been one shitty day.'

Arvid giggles. 'Why not?' he says. 'It is Friday and all.'

We walk into the shopping centre from the top level along the square towards the door to Geir's. Arvid carries his rucksack in his hand. On his back, it would make him look like a schoolboy, and we open the door, walk in and sit down at a table right at the back.

'I hate to tell you, I'm skint,' he says, 'but if I dig around I may have enough for one.'

'Hell, it's on me.' I order two beers. There are some things with alcohol you must never do. You must never drink alone, never drink on Sundays, never drink before seven o'clock and if you do, it has to be on a Saturday. If you're hung-over, you go for a walk in the forest, and you must never drink the hair of the dog. Do that, and you are an alcoholic, it's common knowledge. If you are an alcoholic you're out of control. If you have no control, you are finished. Then you spend the rest of your days walking through the valley of the shadow of death. You are the problem no one wants to solve. They give you a wide berth in the street, scurry behind the canned food when you're in the shop to buy beer. The woman at the cash desk is in a hurry. And then you die and no one gives a shit.

It's not Saturday, and it's well before seven o'clock, but apart from that, we're in the clear, and after the first sip I feel good. Arvid smiles and wipes the froth off his top lip.

'That was good,' he says. 'We ought to do this more often.

69

It's a shame we don't have money, then we could have a few more.'

'You've got the hundred kroner,' I say.

'But of course I do,' he says and grins.

7

I wake up. I have been dreaming about Egil for the first time since the accident. In the dream we are standing on a log by the bank of the river Glomma, fishing with our new spinning rods. We got them for Christmas and haven't tried them out yet. It's Easter, perhaps. The silver reels glisten in the sun, and Egil looks the way he did last year. I know he is dead, but it doesn't matter. It is absolutely still by the river. Straight ahead the water's swirling and further up are the rapids, and yet we do not hear a sound. It is wonderful. Egil smiles and casts a long line, he is happy, and I smile back at him. I can't remember ever seeing him so calm, his face so soft and smooth. He's relaxed because he knows he is no longer alive, and there will be no more trouble. That calms me, too.

The rods are a joy to cast. The spinner flies out towards the middle of the river. I have never cast so far, it just glides of its own accord. I close my eyes and let the sun warm my skin. Suddenly Egil is shouting, his voice is thin. There is something on his hook, and there is fear in his eyes. The old scowl is back. I run over to help him: his rod is bent to breaking point, and I hold him from behind. But when I touch him his body is not the body of a fifteen-year-old boy. He is plump and warm: how strange, I think, and he is winding the reel like a madman. I grab the rod and wind with him. Then he shrivels and fades away, and winding alone is hard work. Suddenly it's as if the river is boiling, and I see the bumper of the Volvo Amazon break the surface, and then the bonnet, and the car pitches like a huge fish with its belly in the air and then I see the windscreen and start to cry.

When I wake up it's dark, and I am still crying. I feel a little sick, and heavy as I roll over and have look at the alarm clock. In half an hour I have to be up and on my newspaper round. I roll back, I want to sleep longer, but when I close my eyes, the car is back, it's in my pillow, it's on the wall, and I can't escape it.

I get out of bed and dress and go down to the kitchen. It's dark down the stairs, and the kitchen is dark and cold, and my body too is cold. My mother is asleep. I leave the light off and go to the stove and lift the lid of the hotplate. We still have it. The plate is set to three, and in the dark the element has a faint glow, you can light your cigarette on it. I turn and lean against the edge and let the heat drift all the way up to my neck. I turn back and give my stomach the same treatment. When we were just kids in the country, Egil always raced to be first down the stairs to the kitchen in the morning. He would pull over a stool and get up on it with his back to the stove and his bum out, and he had such a greedy look on his face. I remember how I didn't like that face, it made me feel embarrassed, and I never tried to fight him for the stool, even though I too was cold in the morning. Now it's only me, and I can stand here for as long as I like.

I fill the kettle and put it on and stand waiting. Outside it's dark, but I can just make out the low-rises in Linderud.

Some windows are lit. It used to be just fields out that way. Arvid flew kites there in the autumn, and horses from the Linderud estate were grazing as far down as Østre Aker vei. Now the Siemens building towers above the road. At the top, close by the large white manor house, is the EPA shopping centre. It looks like shit. There is not a farm worth the name in the valley now. I can't see the forest from the window, our house is too far down in the dip, but I can sense that it's there.

The water is boiling. I take a handful of coffee from the brown tin and drop it in, wait for it to sink, cut two slices of bread and see from the clock above the stove that I have plenty of time. I grab the handle of the kettle and lift it and let the kettle fall a few times to get it going. I try a cup, but it's not there yet. I fetch milk from the fridge, pour a glass and sit down and eat, and by the time I have finished, the coffee is ready. It flows nice and thick from the spout. I hear sounds from my mother's room, she goes to the toilet, and I stand in the dark not moving, afraid she will get dressed and come out. But it goes quiet again. I stay in the dark, roll a cigarette and sit at the table and smoke and drink coffee and look out of the window.

I keep my barrow just behind the stairs at the bottom of the tower. Everybody knows it's mine, I have put my foot down, so the kids don't fool around with it. I pull it out on to the footpath and walk up Beverveien towards the shopping centre. This morning I am the first one there. The newspapers are piled outside the depot, and I load the two packages on to the barrow and cut the strings. I see Fru Johansen coming down the road, but I don't hang around for a chat. I set off along Grevlingveien and at the same time keep an eye peeled for the Vilden family, who are usually the first to arrive, sleepy and dutiful, but today I cannot see them. That makes me feel uneasy, and I know why. It is stupid, but all the same I look back over my shoulder towards the shopping centre as I move down Veitvetsvingen. After the first house where Pål, who used to be in my class, lives I walk on down the hill, and at the end of the road she is standing by the garage, as if she has been waiting for me. Her hair is untidy, she has been crying, and her face is wet and strained.

'It's Tommy,' she says, 'he didn't come home last night. We've been looking for him everywhere.'

I can hear her words, but I am so captivated by her voice, that at first I don't get what she is really saying. She suddenly looks completely resigned, her shoulders sinking, and she wipes her nose with the back of her hand.

'It's Tommy. We can't find him. He's been gone since yesterday.' She's in despair and bursts into tears, and I just look at her. Her hair is dark and curly, flowing everywhere, I want to run my fingers through it, and I raise my hand and stop by the sleeve of her grey duffle coat, and then I suddenly remember that red spot under Tommy's nose. How come I never thought about that before.

'Perhaps he hasn't got such a bad cold after all,' I mumble.

'What did you say?' Her words come out too loud. She senses it herself and scans the deserted street.

'Come on,' I say, 'I don't think you know where to look.'

I leave the barrow and take her with me up the hill I just

came down. Halfway up, I look back down the road to the house where Arvid lives. He is leaning out of the window; it gives me a start, but I keep on going and do not call to him. It's as if everyone is waiting for me. I hurry up the hill with the girl in tow, and I still don't know her name.

We walk past the shopping centre. Konrad comes chugging by with his cap pulled down on his ears, and he waves, and I don't wave back, just march towards the Metro station and round it and into Hubroveien and along the wire fence by the rails towards the next station at Rødtvet.

'Hey, not so fast,' she says behind me, 'where are we going?' But I do not answer, just keep up the same speed along the fence until the path narrows where the slope comes down from Trondhjemsveien towards the Metro line. There is a little dip at the path's end. On the other side of the rails is Fru Karlsen's house. There is no one standing on the step waiting, but I know she is there behind the curtains, and right in front of me in the grassy dip is Tommy, his head resting against the fence. This is where they hang out. I used to look here for Egil. I stop short, and the girl bumps into me from behind, I can feel her against my back.

'Tommy!' she shouts. I bend down and smell the fumes of Lynol: sweet and strong and nauseous, and I almost throw up the way I always did when we had woodwork at Veitvet School and I had to go into the paint room.

'You little shit,' I say. 'You little swine, what the hell are you doing?' I feel the anger inside me, but when she thumps me in the back with her fists, I stop. I grab him under his arms and legs, the yellow-striped jacket is covered in muck. I hold him tight and walk as fast as I can on the path alongside the rails. He is so small, he is as light as anything and thin and cold as ice, and I start to worry and put my ear to his face to listen for his breathing and then he turns his head with eyes closed and rests his cheek against my chest.

'Papa,' he whispers.

'For Christ's sake!' I say, and she hits me again.

They live in Rådyrveien at the lower part of Veitvet. The long apartment block is identical to the one that I live in, and it stands at an angle to the road below where Låke used to have his grocery store. It's closed now, the windows are lined with cardboard and you can see your reflection as you pass. The fields rise up to the left, towards Bredtvet farm and the prison, where the rebel Hans Nielsen Hauge's statue is standing. The Sunday school is there in the hollow by Condom Creek, and a few years ago there was a ski jump behind a hill near Østre Aker vei. I jumped eighteen metres there once and landed face first. Five stitches.

The father stands waiting by the door to the tower, tall and thin, searching the street, and when he sees us coming, he breaks into a run. His eyes are red from lack of sleep, and I pass Tommy to him, and he lifts the boy and holds him in his arms, and says, 'Oh, Jesus.' And he doesn't even look at me, just hurries back down. He staggers on, his long legs teeter, he looks like a stork with a giant baby in his beak and Tommy's feet are dangling down by his hips.

'Maybe you should call an ambulance,' I say to his sister, 'he's not in great shape.' She nods, and suddenly I feel naked without Tommy in my arms. I turn and look up the street.

'I guess I have to be off. The people waiting for their papers will be pissed off.'

'I know,' she says with a little smile and puts her arms around me and gives me a kiss on the cheek. 'Thank you,' she says. My hands hang down by my side, there is no room for them anywhere, and then she lets go and runs down the road after her father.

When I am almost up to my barrow, old Abrahamsen is standing there, shifting his weight from foot to foot, peering left to right, and then he spots me hurrying up the hill by the Veitvet waterfall and calls from a distance:

'Can I have one?!'

'Sure!' I shout back, even though I am quite close now, and there is no other sound.

'Damn,' he says, 'I won't make it to the bus.' He is really pissed off, but still he doesn't move. I don't know what he wants, and all of a sudden I feel weary.

'Well, run off then, or read *Arbeiderbladet* instead, hell, I don't know, but I just can't stay here.' I take the barrow and set off and then, damn me, if he doesn't go all friendly.

'Look, Audun,' he says, and I turn and he says: 'Well Audun, I've watched you walking this round for several years, and I was wondering. How are you really doing?' He blushes, the old man, and I blush, too, I don't know how to answer a question like that, so I shrug and wait. He scratches his chin, and there is a rasping sound.

'Well, if there is ever anything, you know where I live.' He is relieved; he has said what he wanted to say. He opens the newspaper, and now suddenly he has all the time in the world, and he strolls up the hill past the red telephone booth, and I think to myself, I really don't get this man. He reads while he is walking, he must have radar or sonar navigation, like a bat at night, because he moves between the posts and the bushes by the kerb without once looking up.

I finish off Veitvetsvingen as quickly as I can, and only Grevlingveien is left. People are standing on their steps, waiting, and they are not happy. But I don't look at them or apologise or anything, just push the paper into their hands and hurry on. At the end of the route, by the last house, Fru Karlsen is standing by her door. The dress she is wearing is really something, her shoulders still tanned after the summer have a faint glow, warm, as though she is just out of bed, and I have pictured it white and white, and myself in it, and my own skin close to the skin I can see now, her hands everywhere, and my hands everywhere, where she is soft and different, and the dizzying fragrance of Fru Karlsen, but straight away I can see that there is something amiss, for her arm is rigid as she runs her hand through her hair, and I just want to turn and get the hell out of there. But I can't, I have to give her the newspaper, it's my job, and I walk slowly towards her on the flagstone footpath.

'Well, if it isn't Speedy Gonzales,' she says. Her mouth is distorted in a way I have never seen before, and I pass her the newspaper. She doesn't take it, doesn't look at it, her eyes are glaring straight at me. It makes me feel uncomfortable.

'What the hell do you mean by being late when you know I am waiting for you! Can't you see I'm all dressed up?' She seems a little drunk, but she can't have been drinking, it's barely half-past six, and yet, there is this shine in her eyes, and she looks cold wearing that dress well into October. She is freezing, and she has dressed herself up for me.

'Things happened on the way round, I had to sort that out first. You're not the only person who is pissed off.'

'The only person! You foolish boy! You could have had anything you liked! Do you understand what I'm saying? I could have given you anything you liked! But I am not waiting for anyone, especially not a baby like you!' And then she slaps me. There is no time to duck, and it stings like hell. I back a few steps, squeeze the newspaper hard, it's thick today, and heavy, and I sling it at her. It hits her where she is really soft. Whether it hurts or not I cannot tell, but she is startled, her eyes change colour, and I say in a low voice:

'You old hag! Get back inside to that old man of yours! I wouldn't touch your wrinkled skin if you paid me!'

8

We have French for the first lesson. Henrik has to read aloud from the text we've had to prepare. He sits at the very back. He can't do French, neither reading nor writing it, but he is a good imitator. That's what he can do, and with a little help he has bluffed his way through two years, and is close to the abyss. If we have a French oral, he is done for. But Starheim is hard of hearing, he leans forward with a cautious smile, his eyes glued to Henrik's face. It sounds like French, he is almost certain. Everyone can see he really doesn't catch *what* Henrik is reading, but it does sound French, and Henrik throws his whole body into it, so it *looks* French as well. Henrik really doesn't say anything, it's just babble, but Starheim is vain, he won't be caught saying *what?* or *eh?* so he just goes for it:

'Très bien, merci, Henri. Audun, you can take it from there.'

I have no idea where Starheim thinks Henrik stopped reading, so I choose a place at random and keep going. Henrik's face is like a mask, and Starheim does not bat an eyelid. I used to think this was funny. I have done my homework, I understand what I am reading, but my pronunciation is not great, and it's enough for Starheim to smile with relief and say:

'Pas mal, Audun. A little more practice on your

pronunciation, and you'll be fine.' Henrik looks triumphant, this is killing him, his face tense and almost desperate and his eyes filled with tears. Tiny sounds come from his mouth. He can't hold it back much longer. A few students have to look out the window.

'Not bloody likely,' I say under my breath, so only those next to me can hear.

On our way out Arvid says:

'Henrik's skating on thin ice. I don't think the examiners are quite as deaf. But it's funny.'

'I don't understand why he bothers.'

'What's the matter with you? You knew your stuff, didn't you.'

'Nothing's the matter with me. I'm just a little tired.' I close my eyes and see Fru Karlsen and her face when the newspaper hit her. Arvid pats my shoulder. I feel like telling him about Fru Karlsen, but all that's another world.

'Have you heard about the Stakhanov Prize?' he says. 'It was a prize Stalin gave to the most industrious workers during the first five-year plan. It was named after a man who worked his ass off. You're in the semi-finals.'

We walk across the schoolyard between students from our class, and we stand in the sun with our backs to the gymnasium. I look around me, and then I turn the corner where there is nothing but trees and sit down on the grassy slope leading up to the teachers' houses and fish out half a cigarette from my pocket and light it up. I sit smoking in the strip of sunlight with my eyes closed. Arvid follows me.

'Give us a drag,' he says. I pass him the cigarette. He

inhales, and then he slowly blows out smoke and looks at me.

'Seen any more of your dad?'

I shake my head.

'Weird business,' he says, and that's all he *can* say, because it's something he doesn't understand. It's not his fault, I know that, but still it's irritating.

'It'll be fine,' I say.

'I hope so.' He gives me back my cigarette, and I take the final drag just before I burn my fingertips, and I am about to throw it away, when a head pokes round the corner.

'Gotcha!' I drop the butt and stamp on it. It's Twisty, one of our teachers. He is called Twisty because of the way he walks, but it is meant kindly, he is well liked by all the students. He walks all the way round and says:

'Shit, do you have to smoke when I'm on duty? You'll get me into trouble. Look here,' he says, putting a hand up his jacket, 'the new polec booklets have come.'

He is a SUF-er, a Young Socialist member, they have their own lingo and 'polec' means political economy. Arvid has joined a study group. He is eager, he grabs the booklet, and Twisty reaches for another.

'Are you joining as well?' he says to me. 'We start on Tuesday.'

I shake my head.

'He's not ripe yet,' Arvid says, 'but he will be, don't push him.'

'That would be great,' Twisty says. 'Do you know, Arvid, the membership of the NLF group has doubled since the stunt with the flag? That was a class act.' Arvid blushes, and I agree. It *was* a class act.

'I have to be off. The bell will go in a couple of minutes. No more smoking, please.' He twists back around the corner, and we get up and brush the pine needles off our trousers.

'This is not for real,' I say.

'What isn't?'

'All this. Henrik with his French, Twisty and his booklets, the whole school.'

'Sure it is,' Arvid says.

We have Rønning, the deputy headmaster, for English. He is the only teacher I like. He is sort of a show-off in his West-Norwegian way, parading the classroom pulling at his red braces, his jacket dangling from his shoulders, his grey hair whirling round his head, and he speaks English with a heavy Stord Island accent. He loves for us to laugh at his jokes, but we don't understand them. He is passionate about his subject, though, and feeds us extra reading; in his office the spirit duplicator works overtime. It will soon be on its knees with metal fatigue. When he comes down the corridors, a cloying smell of spirit drifts behind him.

Our textbook is the *Anglo-American Reader*. The English in it is tiresome, with a faint taste of bog water at the edges, but the American has a sky above it that I feel comfortable with. We are reading about the Melting Pot. The Golden America, the land of freedom and equality, the haven for the homeless and persecuted, the melon they all want a slice of, the fields they all want to plough. Poor folk from

Hardanger in Norway, the Abruzzi in Italy, and the Ukraine fleeing from landowners, Cossacks and the taxman, the bastards who bleed the smallholder dry until there is nothing left to eat except granite, and if you are not an Indian or a Negro, you may have a chance to see a future ahead of you and a patch of land on the prairie. I am not an idiot, I know about the napalm in Vietnam, I know about Wounded Knee and the Ku Klux Klan; for as long as I have lived I have seen the race riots on TV. They shot Martin Luther King and Malcolm X, I have read Eldridge Cleaver's *Soul on Ice* and felt the flames of his hatred. But there is something about those people. They are for real. They step out of the shadows and set out on journeys never to return. A girl in the book writes about her grandmother coming to America on board the SS *Imperator* sailing past the Statue of Liberty to Ellis Island. There is winter in the air, and she walks down the gang plank in her colourful clothes and her black hair to the gates where the wheat is separated from the chaff, snowflakes drifting, and she is cold and the girl writes: *the snow like stars in the night of her hair*. She is happy with that sentence, and so am I. I turn to Arvid and say:

'Isn't it good?' He reads the piece twice and looks up at me.

'Purple prose,' he says.

'What the hell do you mean by that?'

'Too much. Sentimental. US propaganda.'

'But, for Christ's sake, don't you get it? Those people just took off, burned all their bridges and this girl is trying to show how afraid they were, and at the same time how grand their deed was.'

'Maybe, but it's still purple prose.'

I snatch the book back.

'Sometimes, Arvid, Christ,' I say, and read on to myself. Maybe he is right, maybe it is purple prose, but I like it.

'Is what you're doing of any importance to the rest of us?' Rønning says. He's standing by the dais with his thumbs tugging at his braces, gazing down the row of desks.

'There was just something in the text. I thought it was good. I didn't mean to interrupt.'

'I see. Perhaps you might like to read it aloud for us?' It's like he's rolling his 'r's even more than usual today. I look at him pleadingly, but he grins and splays his hands. Hell. I read. I read the whole page and finish with that sentence, the grandmother almost chokes me, my voice cracks, and everyone turns to look at me. I'm supposed to be the tough guy in the class, the strongest, the best athlete and generally as dour as shit. It just turns out that way, I don't know why. I stare back, they think I am strange, it's fine by me, they're like mist, I hardly see them. Arvid's and Venke's faces are the only ones I can really make out. There is a shine in Venke's eyes.

'That's not bad at all,' Rønning says.

'Forget it,' I say.

After the lesson Rønning stops me at the door. He waits until everyone has left and says, 'I am sorry. I shouldn't have pushed you into reading aloud. I wasn't aware it meant so much to you.'

'It doesn't matter.'

'Well that's good then. Is everything OK with you? You have been a little, what shall I say, reserved these days.' He smiles. I shrug.

'I think maybe I'm going to stop coming here.'

'Now? Well into your final year? Well, school isn't everything. Don't think I believe that. There are many other things you can do. Perhaps you need a break. Sleep on it for a week, then come to me, and we can talk about it.'

'OK, that's fine,' I say.

'By the way, I have a book at home about Ellis Island. It might be of interest to you.'

9

When we put Egil in his grave, it was Easter. Kari was supposed to move to Kløfta the week before. There had been some fine days, it was spring for real, nature was going berserk, and her boyfriend was standing in the sun outside the block with his lorry waiting. He couldn't be bothered helping us, and that was just fine with me. I couldn't stand either him or his lorry. I went to my room to fetch something I had bought for Kari, an old Supremes album I had got hold of at Ringstrøm's Records, and I was standing by the window looking down at him. He was leaning against the red bonnet smoking, flicking the ash from his cigarette, and running his hand through his Brylcreemed hair. Then he stubbed out the butt on the footpath and looked up at the windows with sleepy eyes and a sullen smile. He was James Dean, and he had made this long trek to rescue Kari from suburban hell.

Egil came out of the stairway and walked up to the lorry with a large box in his arms. He'd been in a lot of trouble over the last year, and now he had stayed close to home for a while, but I could see how he was restless, he had this scowl on his face. He shoved the box on to the back of the lorry and the two of them started chatting. Egil was keen and unable to stand still, and after a few minutes he was sitting behind the wheel and had started the engine. It began to roll down Beverveien and rounded the bend at the end of the road. When I came out with Kari, he had driven the whole loop and was on his way back down from the top. I gave Kari the record.

'Here you are,' I said. 'Listen to this and dream about the old days.' She looked at me in surprise and was so happy that she hugged me right in front of her boyfriend.

'Silly you. Thank you so very much. You think of everyone, don't you?'

'Yuk,' I said. I didn't want anyone to think that about me. It wasn't even true. But she was my sister, and she had always been OK.

'Don't get married straight away,' I said. 'Think about it first,' and she laughed, but her boyfriend sneered, and when the lorry was back in place, I walked up close to him and brushed him pretty hard with my shoulder as I hurled a bag of clothes on to the back.

'Hell,' he said, and spun round, but I didn't even look at him, just kept him behind me, and he had to stand there panting on his own.

Egil stepped out of the cabin. He was excited, his whole body shaking.

'Cool wheels,' he said, gazing at Kari's guy as though he really *was* James Dean, and right away James Dean was in a much better mood and combed his hand through his greasy hair and said:

'Of course it's cool, I fixed it and did the paint job myself. You know, Egil, if it's a job you're after, there's enough to do around my place.'

'Do you mean that?' Egil said, and was even more excited.

'Dead right I do. You're a natural.' He gave a generous swing of his arm, and glanced at me.

Egil turned. 'Did you hear that, Audun?'

'Sure I did. You're welcome!' I said and walked straight to the stairway and didn't look back. That was the last thing I said to him. I met my mother on my way up. She was crying because Kari was moving out.

'Is something the matter?' she sniffled.

'No. I'm just getting the last few things.'

Egil went with them up to the country to help unload the truck and have a look at the place where he might be working. He didn't come back. Two days later he drove one of James Dean's Volvo Amazons into the river Glomma and drowned.

On Good Friday, spring was cancelled and the next day the sleet came. It stuck to our faces as we came out of the church with the coffin between us. I had thought it would be heavier. I was holding one handle, and behind me came Arvid and behind him it was Kari. On the other side was my mother, and behind her Roberto, and last came Egil's teacher from school. He had stood up for Egil many times, had pleaded for him when he broke into the Co-op, but it was no good. Egil had been his special vocation, and now it was over.

There was no one else. JD said he didn't feel too good, so he stayed in bed back at Kløfta and drank blackcurrant toddies. It was fine by me. There had been talk about letting my father know, but I refused and said if he showed his face I would take off into the woods and stay there until he had left.

The priest was bad. He had been to our flat to offer his comfort and ask about Egil and what he was like, so he could prepare his talk for the church. He was the priest, so we told him the truth, he had been a pain in the ass, and when we were halfway through the truth, he got up from the sofa and took his coat.

'OK, that's enough. I think I will do it my way.'

And he did. Nothing of what we had told him was included. Just some waffle about the shining light he had been to those around him, how his youthful vigour had been brought to such a sudden end and then the after-life with its eternal restoration, sunshine beyond compare and twittering of birds, and I just switched off, my mother stopped crying and Kari sat staring up at the ceiling. Not a tear between us.

'What a sack of shit, he is,' Arvid whispered behind me as we came out into the slush and laid the coffin on the long trolley and started hauling it across the gravel. 'He got Egil mixed up with Little Lord Fauntleroy.'

I didn't answer, I did not even think, just looked down at my shoes and tried to steer the coffin, and then I looked at the trees that were covered by white curtains, and we followed the priest on his way to the open grave. The air was full of flakes that came down upon us, and when I stared up at them, it felt as if we were running, and that was exactly what I was thinking, that I would run away from all this. We were moving slowly towards the grave, and when finally we got there and were about to lift the coffin from the trolley, I had to look down. There was sleet at the bottom of the grave and water and wet clay. It looked cold and awful and I remembered the Easter when Egil and I had been poaching in a reservoir north of where we lived. Three perch we caught, and there were more there for the taking. We had sneaked out early, my father was still asleep, so I reckoned we would be all right. Egil was just a kid, but he was a demon at fishing, and I was sure that his eagerness to do it again was so great that he would keep his mouth shut. The plan was to hide our rods in the woodshed on the way back and say we had been playing cards at my pal Frank's house because Good Friday was so boring. So my father thought too, and he was a keen poker player. The fish we had already given away to a woman we met on the road. We liked fishing, but we didn't like fish. The problem was that Egil had stumbled into the lake, he was soaked to the knees, and I still had the rods under my arm when we walked up the path from the gate.

He was standing on the steps in his underwear, his head tilted and his hands down by his sides.

'Come here, Egil,' he smiled. Egil grinned with relief and went over to the steps. My father tousled his hair, and Egil leaned against his hip.

'Where've you been so early, Egil?'

'We've been playing cards at Frank's house.'

'You don't say. And you dropped the cards in the swimming pool, did you, and you had to wade in after them?'

Egil laughed. 'Frank hasn't got a swimming pool, you know that.'

'Wow, you don't say? Where the hell have you been fishing then?' my father said and hurled Egil against the wall. I felt the thump through my whole body and Egil was winded, he turned white and then he began to sob.

'Now watch carefully, Egil,' my father said. 'Audun, come here.' I looked at him. I put down the rods and took the box of bait and the extra hooks from my pocket and put them down too before I walked towards the steps. It was a distance of ten metres, and I took my time. I motioned to Egil to keep his mouth shut, and the minute I turned round, my father's hand came out of nowhere and hit my face. I was knocked backwards and my cheek went numb, I couldn't feel a thing and then it went hot and then there was a pain.

'Are you watching carefully, Egil?'

'Yes,' Egil said.

I rose to my knees, I thought, I'm getting out of here, and then he lashed out again and hit me on the side of the head and my ears were ringing and I could barely hear Egil shouting:

'We were fishing in the reservoir! That's what we were doing, but it was Audun's idea. It was. Cross my heart.'

I was ten years old at the time, Egil was eight and when school started after the Easter holidays I was still in bed, and every move I made was painful. Now the sexton was turning the crank and the coffin sank into the earth. Kari threw a bunch of roses and the priest threw soil. I turned and walked up to the church and out through the gate and stood outside on the road smoking and trying to think, but everything I touched was oily and just slipped out of reach.

Sleet gave way to rain. I held the cigarette in the hollow of my hand, and my confirmation coat had grown too small, it made me feel fat, it annoyed me, and then they were finished over in the cemetery. The small flock came slowly up to the gate and there they stopped, and the priest shook their hands one by one and said a few words. I couldn't hear him, but the look on his face was mild and sympathetic, and eventually he came up to me and said:

'So, you didn't want to pay your brother your final respects?'

'You don't know what you're talking about,' I said. We were the same height and looked each other straight in the eye.

'I know that when this life is over and the next begins, then there shall be peace,' he said, and he was clearly pleased with his words. I looked into his face. If ever I wanted to punch someone, that would be now.

'Kiss my arse,' I said.

10

It's Friday. Arvid calls and wants me to go with him to the club. He sounds worked up. I am tired, I sleep badly, and when I can't sleep, I read. I have started Hemingway and Arthur Omre, but it's too much. After the newspaper round and school, my brain is spinning. Still I say yes.

The club is in the shopping centre on the second level, and the entrance is right behind the spiral staircase leading up to the third. The staircase is a free-standing tower with a footbridge from the top to the market square, and Olav Selvaag, the entrepreneur, liked the tower so much that when Veitvet was finished he used it as a logo, and all his vehicles have it painted on the door.

An electric sign says Linderud Youth Club, even though Linderud is the next station. It's childish, I know, but it has always annoyed me, and when I come up the slope by the post office and the music school, Arvid is standing by the staircase waiting. Several young people walk past him on the way in, but Arvid's leaning against the railing, smoking in his yellow cord trousers and black jacket. Under the jacket he has a Fair Isle sweater and a large loose scarf round his neck. His hair is long now, if that's the way to say it, because his curls grow out in all directions, and he is wearing a beret, which his grandfather gave him for Christmas last year. It's not often he has the nerve to wear it.

He looks cool. The girls in his class dig him, but he is so shy he doesn't get it, and that's why it all comes to nothing. I may be wrong, though. Perhaps he doesn't tell me everything, I don't tell him everything, but what I do know is that everyone who passes through the door into the club is at least two years younger than we are, and I don't understand what we're doing here. It's a year since we last came, and I said a sleepy yes on the phone because it seemed important to him.

I walk up to him and say:

'Hell, Arvid, all they do in there is play table tennis and dance, and they dance like shit to music we hate. And I don't even like table tennis.'

'We're not staying. We'll be off after a while.'

'So why go at all? It's not even certain they'll let us in. We're over eighteen.'

'Just for a little while.'

I should have stayed home. I should have lain down for an hour to sleep off the anxious feeling that's in my stomach, but then they do let us in. The club leader is standing in the doorway looking sceptical, he is closer to us in age than most of the kids who hang out at the club. He stops us and asks how old we are. It's embarrassing.

'Eighteen.'

'When?'

'Just turned.'

'OK, but we don't want any trouble. You haven't been to Geir's bar first, have you?'

'Are you crazy?'

'And no fooling with the girls.'

We go in, and I stop in the middle of the hall. 'Shit, Arvid, I'm not up for this.'

'Just for a little while.'

The place is packed to the rafters. All the rooms are crowded with people, and I don't know what to do with myself, so I stand in a doorway watching some snot-nosed kids playing table tennis. Arvid has gone off after checking out the room. The discotheque is right at the back, the music banging into the hall every time someone opens a door, and many turn to look at him as he hurries further in. He has shoved his beret into his jacket pocket, but still he looks cool.

Most people in the room I have seen before, but I don't really know them, and many look up at me in surprise, and one calls out:

'Hey, Audun, I thought you'd retired?' His name is Willy, and he is one of those who hang around the Metro station. He is sixteen and was a friend of Egil's. I always thought he was a slimy bastard. Whenever he came to our door to ask for Egil, I left him standing outside on the Sing-Sing gallery, even when it was pelting down.

I shrug and look past him and see Tommy's sister sitting in a corner talking with two other girls. She looks back at me, and I blush, and Willy puts down his table tennis racket and carves his way through. He comes straight over to me and smiles. I can't for the life of me think why: maybe because I am the oldest person in the room, and he wants to impress. He has shoulder-length blond hair, a little longer than mine, and he takes hold of my arm and says:

'Shit, Audun, that was a bloody shame about your brother. Egil was a dead cool guy.'

I remove his hand. 'Beat it,' I say.

He doesn't like that. He gets confused and looks round to see who has heard what I said, but the table tennis balls click to and fro, and sometimes they bounce on to the floor, and the players shout and laugh and are having a good time.

'Come on, Audun, surely I have a right to say something. Shit, Egil was my best friend.'

'Did you hear what I said? Scram!' I push him away, he staggers backwards, and now it's hard for him to pretend nothing is happening. The room goes quiet, and those inside it turn and look to the doorway where I am standing. It's fine by me. I have no business with them. Willy crouches down and gets sly, he smiles, he wants to fight, one word from me, and he will fight. That's fine, too, I don't give a shit, and then Arvid comes down the hall, his face in a frenzy.

'They're not here,' he says.

'Who isn't?'

'Unless you're one of them?' he says and walks straight up to Willy and slams him against the wall.

'Hey, give me a break,' Willy says, 'I had nothing to do with it!'

I am completely at sea. Arvid suddenly goes wild, his thin body tense like a wire, he can't keep his feet down, and he grabs Willy around the neck and pins him to the wall.

'One of who, Arvid?'

'One of those who beat up my dad. Just two hours ago. He was on his way home from his shift, right, and when he came out of the Metro, this gang went for him. I guess he didn't think their jokes were funny. How the hell would I know! And now he's at home in bed, and he looks a mess.' He starts shaking Willy like a rag doll, and I don't understand why Willy is just standing there looking scared instead of fighting back. He must be stronger than skinny Arvid and much more used to a scrap, but he shouts:

'I wasn't with them. It was Dole and the others.'

'Dole and the others? For fuck's sake, Dole is your great pal, isn't he? You knucklehead!' Arvid yells, and now he is pounding Willy, and it looks so awkward, and no one is playing table tennis any more, they're all on their feet roaring and cheering, and I grab Arvid's shoulder and haul him off, and in the corridor I can hear the club leaders come running. We have to get out, pronto. I hold his shoulder in a rock-hard grip and hiss in his ear:

'Calm down for Christ's sake. We're leaving.' The man at the door rounds the corner and blocks the exit. I move in close, wrap my arms round his back, and before anyone can see what I am doing, I lift him and carry him into the next room. There he stands yelling in the middle of the floor.

'You just wait! I'll get you for this!'

'Kiss my arse,' I say and pull Arvid by the jacket and run down the hall and out through the door. It's dark outside and suddenly cold, and we carry on up the spiral staircase, round and round, and into the square. There we stop, and I say: 'What the hell has got into you? Why can't you tell me what's going on before you drag me out? And here I was, convinced it was a girl you were after, the way you'd dressed up!'

'You have to show them who you are, don't you get it?'
He snatches the beret from his pocket and smacks it on his
head. He hasn't calmed down at all, my friend is standing
there shouting into my face.

'He's sixty years old, for Christ's sake, and he doesn't
even admit it to himself. He was a boxer, right, he still
believes he's young, and now he's been beaten up by a gang
of snot-nosed kids. He doesn't even dare to go to casualty
although he needs stitches all over his face. He *crawled* up
the stairs, goddamnit. Do you understand what shape he's
in?'

'Hell, of course I do, just calm down a bit,' I say, but I
don't understand what shape Arvid's father is in, I only
know that I am getting angry too. His father's been beaten
up, it's a disgrace, but why does he have to shout at me?
'No need to get hysterical. Calm down,' I say again.

'Why should I calm down? Tell me why I should calm
down!' He is close to tears, and suddenly he pokes me in
the chest. 'Tell me why I should calm down!' he shouts.

'Take that stupid beret off,' I say. 'It looks so goddamn
pretentious!' He stands in front of me, his mouth wide open,
and I really feel like punching him. But of course I can't,
and I don't know where to put my hands, but I will hit him
unless I can think of something very quickly. I don't want
to beat it and leave him here alone, and so I do the only
thing I can think of and put my arms around him, pull him
close to me and hold him tight. Very tight. He goes as stiff
as a fence post and gasps for air, and only then do I realise
that Arvid loves his father. It has never occurred to me.
They seem to argue most of the time, they slam doors and

shout at each other up and down the stairs. I am still angry, and I squeeze him, and then Arvid starts crying. For fuck's sake, he says to my shoulder, and he loves his father so much, and now that he's been beaten up, Arvid wants to take on the whole of Veitvet on his own, beret and all. It makes me furious, and I squeeze him harder, and there's a heat surging up from my legs into my stomach, and it's not a nice feeling at all, so I keep it down there, and we stand in the middle of this market square hugging each other, and if anyone sees us now, they're bound to think we are a couple of homos.

I don't know if I dare let him go. If I do, I will feel naked and cold and lost in this world.

Somewhere a clock is ticking. I see the sign for the Skoglund grocery store, I have seen it a thousand times before, but never like this in the midst of a silence. Outside the silence a car comes to a halt and sets off again, and then I hear quick footsteps, someone is moving up behind me and says:

'Hey, I followed you,' and little by little I release him. I don't know how long we have been standing like this, but my arms ache, and I realise that I have been squeezing him as hard as I can. In my chest there is a pain, and Arvid straightens up and takes a deep breath, there is a whistle in his throat, and I see what caused the pain: it's the NLF badge on his lapel. I lean towards him and whisper:

'Forget what I said about your beret, it's just fine.' But he looks at me as though he has never seen me before, I could have been Christopher Columbus and he my first

Indian, his face is flushed and his eyes are shiny. I turn, and it's Tommy's sister standing there.

'What's your name?' I say.

'What?'

'What's your name, for Christ's sake?' I'm almost yelling, but she answers calmly:

'Rita. Didn't you know?'

'No.'

'Right. Well, anyway, I heard what you said at the club. It's true that it was Dole and a few others. Willy just stood watching. Dole's in there,' she says and points. We are standing outside Geir's bar. I look through the window. Dole is sitting at the nearest table with a beer in front of him, it has a golden gleam from the lamp above, and I can see the bubbles from here, and he has a crew cut, like an American marine. He was the first to have long hair at school, and now he has no hair at all. His head is large and round, and he is laughing and telling something funny to someone I cannot see. I turn to Arvid.

'Right, shall we go in then?' I say a bit roughly, but he just looks at me and has no idea what I am talking about.

'What's up with him?' Rita asks. 'Did you have a fight?'

'He's upset about his dad. Don't come with me now.'

I walk towards the bar door. As I'm about to go in, it's pushed open from the inside, and one of the local drunks comes staggering out. I stand back, and Dole looks up and sees me through the window. He knows who I am, but not what I want. I push the drunk aside and clear the way, and inside I head straight for the table where Dole is sitting. He is pretty hammered, he grins and says:

101

'Hello, Audun, old boy,' but I don't answer, I just go up to him, lean down and grab his leg and pull. He hits the floor with a bang, the chair tips forward and hits him on the back of the head, the glass is knocked over and all the beer splashes down on his crew cut. He lashes out with the other leg but I skip to the side, and with his ankle in a firm grip, I drag him to the door.

'Fuck you, Audun! Have you flipped or what!' he yells, and I say nothing, for there is nothing to say, I just drag him along the floor. He flails out on all sides, crashes into chairs and tables, holds on to someone's foot and shouts:

'For fuck's sake, help me!' But no one lifts a finger. I bang open the door with my back, and outside in the square I let go of his leg. He gets to his feet with a groan. Once he has straightened up, I punch him hard in the stomach. I know what I'm doing. I have seen it before. He jack-knifes, and all the beer spurts from his mouth, and it floods out on to the ground between us, and I step away. I stand at the ready. But he coughs and splutters and stares at the tarmac.

'You know what, Audun?' he mumbles. 'You're a dead man.' And then he opens the bar door and walks in bent double.

I turn back to the square. Rita is there alone, watching me with a look in her eyes I could have done without.

'Where's Arvid?' I say.

'He took off. The wrong way, I think.'

Right. I don't know why I did what I did, but I don't think it was for his sake.

'Right,' I say, running my fingers through my hair. I look at her. 'How's Tommy doing?'

'Fine. He's much better now. He really is.'

'Good,' I say, and start towards the stairs.

'Audun?' she says behind me. I turn round. She is wearing a brown leather jacket that must have been passed down from her father, that's how it looks, and she seems older now than I'd thought before.

'Nothing. It's nothing.'

'OK, that's fine then.'

I walk down the spiral staircase and down the slope by the post office and the music school and along the terraced houses in Grevlingveien. It's so quiet. I am breathing calmly. I just feel a little warm in the pit of my stomach. I cross Veitvetveien without looking left or right. A car brakes suddenly, but my eyes are fixed ahead, and I walk the foot-path between the houses until I come out on Beverveien and down to the block where I live.

My mother's in the living room. She is watching TV. On the table there is half a bottle of Upper Ten whisky, and she has her fingers round a glass while she watches Fred Astaire dancing solo across the screen. I have never seen her drunk, but I know she drinks. There are empty bottles stacked behind her winter boots at the back of the cupboard in the hall.

'Hi,' she says without taking her eyes from the TV. 'You're home early. I thought you were going to the youth club?'

'It was boring.'

I'm about to go to my room, but I change my mind and plump down on the sofa. Fred Astaire is sitting in a telephone booth now, talking to Ginger Rogers. He has turned on the French accent, and she doesn't know it's him she is talking to. He gives her some good advice with heavy French 'r's. He pouts. I don't see the point. I get up from the sofa and go over to the cabinet beside the TV and fetch a glass. On the wall above the cabinet is the signed photograph of Jussi Björling.

'Don't mind if I do,' I say in a straight voice. Now she looks up.

'Don't you think we've had enough of that?'

'You're drinking.'

'It's Friday. I've earned it. Well, you're eighteen. You have to find out things for yourself. But be careful. Have some water in it. Here,' she says, pushing over a jug of water. I pour myself a fair amount of Upper Ten and add some water.

'That's Fred Astaire,' she says. 'He could dance with the phone book, and I would watch.' She smiles. She likes having me there. When I am not out, I usually sit in my room listening to records or reading, and she watches TV or listens to an opera in the living room. If she has her music on loud, I turn up the volume as well. I lean back and take a sip. I have never tried whisky before. It doesn't taste good, but it does warm you right down to your feet. I shiver a little. I could get used to this, I think, and then I watch the film. It's completely without meaning, but Ginger Rogers is attractive. She looks intelligent, much more intelligent than the stupid part she is playing. The glass is empty. I am fine now, the shivering has gone. I carefully reach for the bottle and pour myself another one, and she just watches the film. I may as well tell her now.

'I'm quitting school,' I say.

'What?' She tears her eyes from the screen.

'I'm stopping school.'

'Over my dead body.'

'There's nothing to discuss. I have made up my mind.' I take a large swig from the glass, there is not a lot of water in it this time, I swallow and it flows all through my body. I like it, I could sleep now, and Fred Astaire is singing. Ginger Rogers is looking at him, she is smiling, they will find each other in the end. That's good.

I pull myself together.

'We don't have a lot of money, do we,' I say, 'but I can't do both the paper round *and* school any more. If I start working full time, we'll be a lot better off.'

'You don't understand. I get money so you can go to school.'

'What sort of money?'

'It's a state allowance. It's for helping bright children from disadvantaged homes. Or something like that. I don't remember exactly what it's called.' She blushes.

'What! And you've never told me! Why didn't you?'

'That's my business,' she says, glancing at the TV where the credits are rolling. She missed the end of the film.

'I don't care what it's called,' I say, 'I'm going to stop anyway. What's there for me at school? I'm not like the others.'

'Rubbish! What others? Your best friend, Arvid, he's in your class, isn't he? Is he suddenly different from you?'

'Hell, of course he is. Do you want to know what I'm like? Do you want to know what I'm really like?' I get up from the sofa, the room is swaying, I hold on to the table and close my eyes.

'But Audun, are you drunk? How much have you had?' She takes the bottle and checks the contents. The whiskies I took must have been pretty stiff, because there is not much left.

'Forget it,' I say, and let go of the table and head for my room. I trip over the door sill and land on my knees, but that's fine, I was going down there anyway. I pull the accordion out from under my bed and open the case and there it is: black and white with red stripes on the bellows. A Paolo Soprani. I hold it up, put my arms under the straps, loosen the catches on both sides and go back into the living room.

'Goddamnit, now you're going to hear what I'm like,' I say and pull out the bellows and squeeze the keys and the buttons hard at the same time. The accordion sends out a howl that fills the room. I pull and squeeze again, and my mother covers her ears and shouts:

'Audun, what is this? Where did you get that? Answer me!'

'I have thick blood!' I shout and laugh. 'Do you want to hear a tango? Ho, ho! Here's a tango!' I pull and squeeze and stamp my foot, making the whole room shake, the glasses on the table and the glasses in the cupboard clink, and suddenly the picture of Jussi Björling falls off the wall and crashes to the floor. I stop playing and my mother hurries over to pick it up, and then I can see there is a baking recipe on the back and a photo of a loaf. The picture's from a magazine, and the signature is printed on it. I laugh so much I can hardly stand.

III

11

The spring and the summer of the year I was thirteen were sunk in yellow haze. I was sweating all over my body for weeks and weeks and it was hard for me to see clearly. I walked up the gravel path to the house like a drunk, the air about me thick and quivering with a light that could explode at any moment it seemed, and sometimes I would aim for the door and miss. I sat hunched over my school books rubbing my eyes, but the yellow haze would not go away, and I kept going to the kitchen for something to drink. My throat felt so dry, I was constantly thirsty, and in the end I turned away from the school books. When I came home, I took them out of my satchel and the next morning I put them back, but I didn't open them. And I didn't read anything else. The Davy Crockett books were on the shelves, but there was an emptiness surrounding them that made me restless, an emptiness everywhere that made me gasp for air, and I felt sick. I lay in bed for a week gazing at the curtains. They were as sun-yellow as everything else that was on my mind, and outside my head the sticky silence hung thick and hot, and my temperature rose to thirty-nine degrees.

'I have yellow fever,' I said.

'Yellow fever makes your skin go yellow,' my mother said. 'You're poorly, no doubt about it, but if you ask me you look pretty pale.'

'I've definitely got yellow fever,' I said.

'You may have, of course,' she said and went to look it up in the family encyclopaedia, and the symptoms listed there were quite different, but if ever there was something called yellow fever, that's what I had, and no one could tell me different.

After a week I was fed up lying in bed. I got up and put on a baseball cap and sunglasses.

The morning before the last day of school, I woke early, but stayed in bed, gazing at the ceiling, thinking about things. And when my thinking was done, I jumped out of bed and went down to the kitchen where my mother was standing with her forehead against the window looking out at the road.

'Tomorrow I'm going off for a while,' I said.

'Fine,' she said, and was relieved, for she didn't really know what to do with me in the two months that lay ahead of us. She had to work all summer in the cafeteria at Gardermoen airport, and no one had seen my father for months. Kari would work at the newspaper kiosk, and my mother had enough on her plate looking after Egil.

'Where are you going, then?'

'Frank and I are going to the woods, we'll set up camp by Lake Aurtjern. I'll be away for about two weeks.'

'You'll need quite a bit of food then.'

'Not *that* much. We'll do some fishing. Have you got any money?'

'You can have some. I haven't got a lot,' she said, turning her apron pockets inside out, so I could see for myself.

'I'll take whatever you can spare,' I said and tossed the schoolbag over my shoulder, put my sunglasses on and set off for school. She didn't ask which tent we were going to use. We had never owned one; neither had Frank. Besides, I hadn't even spoken to him. We hadn't been friends for a year.

It was quite a trek to school. But that was not where I went. By the chapel, where the roads meet, I turned right towards the railway station. Even that was not a short walk. We lived on the outskirts of the village, and the school and the railway station were at opposite ends.

It was so hot. Not a single leaf stirred on the trees, and sweat ran from my eyebrows over my face, and whenever I moved my arms, my armpits felt raw. Although my schoolbag was half empty, it was painful to carry, so I jumped into a ditch and hid it under a bush. I could pick it up on my way home, or it could just stay there. I really didn't care.

As I walked, my body eased up and gradually the stiffness disappeared, and by the time I reached the station building, I could have run the sixty metres in under nine dead. Perhaps there was something in the air that had changed, I don't know, but still I kept my sunglasses on. I decided to wear them at all times, at least during the day. I liked the distance they created.

For a couple of weeks I had been pestering the manager of the Co-op for his biggest cardboard boxes. Now I had three, and they were really big, I could almost stand upright inside one of them. I had kept them hidden behind a shed, and now I pulled them out and along the railway lines up to some big bushes. There I placed them one against the other, the largest in the middle and cut openings so I could move between all three. I had a hall, a lounge and a bedroom. There was not much space, but it felt right. Then I cut down some twigs from a nearby tree and laid them over the roof as camouflage. On this side of the railway lines there were just fields, so the chances of anyone stumbling upon me were small, and when I crossed the line to the road on the other side, my shack looked just like part of the scrub. I changed a few details and was home at the usual time. There was a large clock on the station building I could see from where I was camping.

I went home empty-handed; my bag was still where I left it, but my mother didn't notice, or if she did, she didn't mention it.

The next day, I packed my rucksack, sleeping bag, blanket for a groundsheet, torch, some extra clothes, fishing rod and the money my mother had given me. Egil stood in the doorway: he wanted to go with me, but she held him by the shoulders so he wouldn't run off, and when I reached the gate I turned, and she looked so small and worn out, and I guessed it wasn't such a bad idea to stay away for a while.

Everything went fine for a few days. The weather held, and that was a good thing, as I wasn't sure at all how the house would cope with the rain. I slept and woke and felt the walls all around me. I could stretch my arms out and touch both ends of the box with my fingers and feel the smooth inside of the cardboard. The sleeping bag was snug and dry, and at night I heard noises that were new to me. There were cars coming and going on the road and the clunk of wheels from passing trains and the screech when a train braked and stopped at the station. I could hear voices, but I was never afraid; all these sounds belonged there, and I could go on sleeping, knowing that this was something I had chosen myself.

I had plenty to read. All newspapers and magazines for the kiosks and the shops were dropped off at the news-stand beside the station, and at the crack of dawn I sneaked over and took the top copies out from under the string of the bound packs, and hoped that the number of copies was on the safe side. I read the left-wing *Arbeiderbladet*, the farmers' *Nationen*, and *Texas* and *Cowboy*, and *Travnytt*, for trotting news. I kept well away from *Romantikk*. When Kari read that magazine, she had a look on her face that made my toes curl.

But mostly I slept. My grandfather used to say you could sleep in your grave. It was something you had to earn, like a legacy, when it was all over. In that case I was taking out an advance on this legacy and withdrew as much as I could, but on the fifth day I woke up and felt good, on top form and all of a sudden very restless. I rolled up the sleeping bag and sneaked over to the tap behind the station, cleaned my teeth and washed my face. The air was chill, the sky overcast and breathing was easy. And yet, in my stomach there was a void that would not go away even after two slices of bread with peanut butter. I took a sweater from my rucksack, put on my sunglasses and started to walk along the silent road by the shops and the railway line, round the long bend and up between the fields by the chapel to the place where our house was. The dew lay shining on everything in sight and made the landscape look moist and grey, and for the first time in a long while, the yellow burning feeling was gone. There was a new shade of green, but my sunglasses made that, and I was used to it.

Not far from home, I rounded a meadow, walked along a rusty barbed wire fence and approached the house from the back. You could take the usual path, but then they could see you from the kitchen window a hundred metres away. I took cover behind a birch tree on the opposite side of the road from our house and stood watching. It couldn't have been later than six. My mother came out of the door with Egil in tow. He was tired and heavy and listless, but she gave him a firm push and closed the door. She didn't lock it, though, so Kari must still have been at home. If I hadn't been standing behind the tree, they would have spotted me; they might have done that anyway, because the birch was not a big birch, but they were in a hurry and just looked straight ahead and rushed down to the main road to catch the Gardermoen bus.

I didn't move. The house looked different. It was still the same, but it was no longer my house, it seemed more distant, as if behind a wall of coloured glass, and I could not go there, because I was on a fishing holiday with Frank by Lake Aurtjern. If Kari hadn't been at home, I could have walked over to the window and looked inside, and there

114

was a good chance that what I saw inside would have been something very different from what I remembered was there just a week ago. But really, it wasn't easy to remember anything, my mind went blank at once, and suddenly my legs began to tremble. It felt as if they could not carry me any longer, so I put my arms around the tree. There was not a breath of wind, but the thin birch was shaking so much, the leaves above me were clattering, and I made up my mind, took a deep breath and set off towards the house on my trembling legs. Then there was the roar of an engine. I turned and looked towards the bus stop. A tractor turned off the main road. It swayed from side to side and slowly came towards me, and then I ran back and hid behind the tree. We were old friends, the tree and I, we were a team. I patted its trunk and stared at the tractor. There was something familiar about the man in the cabin. The left-hand door was missing, and when the tractor came close enough, I could see in, and there sat Kjell from Kløfta. He was one of my father's drinking pals. He was steering with his left hand, in his right he held a green bottle, and after every mouthful he grinned and toasted the shovel that was as high up as it could go and was dangling there, bulky and mud-streaked. A hand stuck out from one side and a black-trousered leg from the other. The foot had no shoe, only the sock emerged, and from where I was standing, it was easy to see that it was not a clean sock. Besides, I had seen it before.

Kjell was almost level with the birch now, above the roar of the engine I could hear him singing Alf Prøysen's *Tango for Two*, and then he turned in to the gate. It was closed, but either he didn't see it, or he couldn't care less, and I heard how the thin, white boards were crushed under the wheels before he took another turn up to the house, lowered the shovel and emptied my father on to the flagstones by the steps.

Kjell put the tractor into neutral, the roar of the engine fell an octave, but it was still as fierce, and with the bottle in his hand he clambered down and went over to the black-clad bundle on the flagstones. He poked my father with his foot, but my father did not stir. Kjell grinned, shrugged, and then he stooped and lifted my father's arm and wrapped it round the bottle so that the green neck stuck up by his cheek, like a baby's feeding bottle. Then he climbed back in, reversed and missed the opening he had already made in the fence and took another chunk of it with him. I stayed where I was until I saw him enter the main road, then warily I set off towards the house.

I didn't go straight there, but stopped by the fence first and looked up at the first floor window. Maybe the tractor had woken Kari. There was no one there, and no one came to open the door. I let go of the fence and circled the house, got closer and he was lying there quite still, no arm, no leg moving, not one black hair ruffled by the wind, and it was not possible to see if he was breathing or not. I was almost certain he was dead. I didn't know what to do. I couldn't knock on the door, couldn't go to Gardermoen to tell my mother, because I wasn't there. For a few moments I didn't move, and I don't think there was a thought in my head. Then I crouched down. His face was brown and thin, and there were furrows down his cheeks and the black fringe hanging over his forehead, the way I had always seen him. Many said my father had style, but to me he looked mean, though not right now, because his fierce blue eyes were closed, and his brow was smooth. I stretched out and touched the lapels of his jacket, felt the rough cloth on my fingertips, and then it happened. He flung himself round and grabbed my wrist and yelled a word I did not understand, he yelled 'MARANA!' and I jerked back and pulled at my hand, but it was too late. He was holding it so hard his knuckles turned white and the skin turned white on his fingers. The bottle fell over, I heard the liquid gurgle and run out on the flagstones as I wrestled and tugged. Whatever it was that had spilled out, it smelt strong and evil, and then I tumbled backwards right into it. I felt sticky and scared, my stomach churned, I was a turtle on its back, and I shouted:

'Let me go, let me go!' I slung my legs in the air, took aim and kicked my heels against his arm with all my force. He groaned and had to let go, and I got to my feet and half stumbled, half ran towards the smashed gate, jumped over the debris. and when I looked back at the house, I saw Kari up in the window. She was still in her dressing gown, she raised her arm and her eyes met mine behind my sunglasses. I stopped. I was about to point and say something, but then instead I shouted:

'KARI!' But it was no good. My father was on his back now with his arms stretched out, his blue eyes gleaming, and I turned and kept running, down the road and all the way to the railway station.

12

I ran and the sun came out as I ran and the clouds dispersed. The grey turned yellow and green, and suddenly it was hot and sweat was running down my back, in my armpits, in my groin and behind my sunglasses, and I thought, I will take them off. But I could not face the sun, I could not stop, I just ran, thinking it was better to run, that I liked running, that I could see everything clearer then and what was behind me would stay behind.

I didn't want to stop, and yet soon I would have to, for I had run past all the fields, past the crossroads by the chapel I had never been in, and then down the entire stretch of the road and into the streets between the houses where people came out to watch me. I saw the railway station ahead of me and people waiting on the platform to go in to work in Oslo. I ran right through the crowd, instead of skirting round them, it would take too much time, and bumped into people without paying heed. One man was shouting after me, but I did not stop to listen to what he was saying or to see who the man was, so his words were left there, hanging in the air before they fell to the ground and were gone, and I ran on along the rails until no one could see me any more and through the bushes to my cardboard house. It was still there, and I had no idea why I thought it would be gone.

I collected my things. I found the torch and the books, stuffed the blanket and clothes into my rucksack and rolled the sleeping bag into a tight bundle before strapping it in its place under the flap, and carried the whole lot to one side. In a rucksack pocket I found some matches, a big box decorated with red felt on the top and small shiny baubles the way you do in kindergarten to make your parents happy. I had made it myself and no one had ever touched it, it had been buried under some junk in a kitchen drawer. Now I was the first one to use it. I walked over to the cardboard house. It had not rained for weeks, so the cardboard was bone dry, and when I struck a match and held it close, it caught fire at once.

In the evening a bonfire can be nice and bright in the darkness, but during the day it is different. Whoosh it went, and within a few minutes the whole house was ablaze. The heat was intense, and I stepped back. When the bushes also caught fire my first thought was to run to the station and get water from the tap at the back, but there were people all around, and I had nothing to say to them. So instead I stood still watching the flames. They rose higher and higher as they spread to the bushes, and I guess they could be seen from a long way away, if anyone cared to look.

'Kiss my arse,' I said, and swung the rucksack on to my back. I set off, giving the station as wide a berth as possible. I waded through knee-high grass wet with dew along a path only we kids knew about, and then I was back on the main road. At the crossroads by the chapel, I didn't go straight on as I usually would have. Instead I turned left on to a gravel road that at first was winding its way between the green fields of barley and then through a cluster of trees and on to places I had never been to before.

I walked for most of the morning. As the hours passed by, the landscape turned hilly and rolling, and all the hollows that cut across the path I was taking never ran in the same direction. Downhill it was easy to walk, but my rucksack felt heavy as lead against the small of my back on the way up again, and I didn't dare stop and take it off until I was certain that what I saw round about was all new to me. And yet I kept seeing familiar things: a crag, a red house, a fence that had collapsed into disrepair. The straps were gnawing the flesh off my shoulders, and I put my thumbs under them to relieve the pressure, and that worked fine for a mile or so, but then that too became painful.

The sun rose and stayed high in the sky. The air was dry in my mouth, and with each step the dust came whirling up from the gravel road. On the track behind me, I could see my footprints like two straight lines in the thick dust, and if I didn't keep my mouth closed, the dust would crunch between my teeth. At the top of a rise I finally stopped. I really needed a drink.

I didn't have the strength to walk one step more. I looked around me. Across the little valley ahead, on the next peak, I could just make out a yellow barn behind a grove of birch trees. It stood out, the yellow was shrill and very unusual. I had never seen a yellow barn in my life, and I thought maybe I could get some water there. I had never been here before, so I guessed it was safe.

Briskly I set off downhill. The road curved down the slope, and I heard the river before I saw it. I walked faster even though the soles of my feet were burning as if someone had rubbed them with a grater, but I didn't care. At the very bottom and around the bend, the river came flowing out of the green shadows between the trees and then into rapids, and the boulders whipped the water into a froth that curved under a bridge, and then the river spread, and there was a deep pool where the water gently whirled before shooting off again over wet, shiny boulders that looked like huge marbles.

That pool looked good.

To get there I had to leave the road, clamber down an incline and over a barbed wire fence. I slid down, took off my rucksack and threw it over the fence. I took a running jump, I was flying, and then I was over. I picked up the rucksack and held it in my arms the last few paces, underneath the bridge on the warm rocks and over to the still water and put it down, avoiding the cowpats. I scouted around. All I could see was a few cows. Not a soul in sight. I took off my sunglasses and all my clothes and stacked them in a pile and went naked over to the pool. I didn't wait, I didn't count, I just jumped in.

It was cold as hell.

Suddenly, and just like in the books, I felt a claw around my chest. I sank, I couldn't move, the water was deep, and I felt my body starting to spin. This can't be true, it's too short a life, I thought, I am only thirteen, for Christ's sake, and then I kicked for all I was worth, but the current was strong and I was pulled into it, my body spinning like a log. I couldn't hold my breath for much longer, and then my hand hit a rock. I took hold and crouched round what air I had left and put my feet against the rock and kicked off and suddenly there was sun and dazzling yellow foam, and I drifted on to the next rock, and it was towering above me, and I clung to it and took breath after deep breath and gazed towards the bank. I was halfway out in the river, but the bank was not that far. I could make it. The cows lay chewing and watching me, their eyes large and round like vacant mirrors. I was nothing to them. OK, I thought, and then I jumped, and again it was cold, and there was a roar in my ears, I held my head high and swam with all my might, staring at the cows that glided past all too quickly.

'Shit!' I yelled and maybe it did some good, for soon I had solid ground under my feet and I could stagger on to dry land. Rotting branches and jagged stones dug into my feet, but I didn't feel any pain.

Slowly I climbed the bank up to where my clothes were piled. My body was still cold, and my legs were heavy, I didn't have the strength to run. There was a large cowpat, and I stopped right in front of it and stood there for a good while before deciding to walk around it on the right-hand side. When I got to my things, I lay face down on the grass. I can dry off in the sun, I thought, I will just lie here and rest a little, and then I'll go on.

When I awoke I was lying in a room with a skylight in the ceiling. The air was grey, like smoke, and a narrow beam of light came down from above. The ceiling was grey and the walls grey. There was no door to the room, but I saw the railings of a staircase coming up in a corner. I ran my hand over my body, and I was naked under the duvet. It too seemed grey, and the faint light was a delicate light and as soft as the duvet, and everything seemed soft in here.

Slowly I rolled over, and my body felt very heavy, and through a window right down by the floor I could see a small part of the yellow barn. Beside the bed was a bucket. I had thrown up in it. I could not remember when. I checked to see if I felt sick, but I didn't. Only very heavy. I closed my eyes.

The next time I awoke, I heard footsteps on the stairs. I opened my eyes and it was darker now, and I could barely make out a woman coming up behind the railing. She was a large woman and light footed, and her hair was dark in the darkness, and she was coming towards me. She stopped beside my bed and took the bucket and carried it to the stairs. She moved without a sound. I watched her through half-open eyes, pretending to be asleep. Then she came back, dipped her hand in her apron pocket and put something on a shelf by the bed.

'What's that?' I said.

'It's your sunglasses. You were shouting and making such a terrible fuss about them that Leif went back to the river and found them where your clothes were.'

'Did I shout?'

'It can't be denied.'

'I don't need them now. It's so dark in here.'

'That's good. How are you?'

'I feel heavy.'

She smiled. 'I guess you do. Look here now,' she said and bent over me and pulled the pillow out and shook it and put it back behind my head. Her breast brushed against my cheek. It was large and soft. She straightened up. I closed my eyes.

'Go back to sleep,' she said.

'Right.'

She walked without a sound towards the staircase, took the bucket and started down the steps. I could see her face. It wasn't that round, and soon she would be all gone.

'Who's Leif?' I said. She turned and smiled. Only her head could be seen above the floor.

'That's my husband. Signe is my name.'

Signe white, Signe soft, blessed Signe, I thought. Bless the day, bless your feet on the path and the light on your brow.

'Get some more sleep. It's night now. You can sleep for as long as you want. It's nobody's business.'

'Right.'

And then she was gone. Everything went quiet again, and when I looked out the window by the floor, the yellow barn had turned grey. I could sleep some more. I could sleep for ever. Just lie here under this skylight and sleep.

The sun shone through the skylight and woke me. Now the whole room was white. I felt listless, but the heaviness was gone. My clothes lay on a spindle-back chair by the bed, and carefully I swung myself out and started to put them on. They were clean and dry. How could anyone have had the time? I thought. The column of light from the ceiling made the duvet and the sheet shine; it looked like something from the Bible we used to read at school. It was fine to look at, but I couldn't stay around, I was famished.

I went to the stairs and tried not to make those creaking sounds on my way down, but it couldn't be done. I came out into a hall with working clothes on hooks in a row, and there was an open door, leading to a room that was filled with light. Inside there was someone humming. I sneaked up to have a look and saw Signe by the worktop holding three large jars. She did not turn, and yet she said:

'Is that the young lad? Don't stand outside freezing!' She laughed with a surprisingly soft, dark chuckle. 'Come in and get yourself something to eat. You must be hungry as a bear. I've just been to the pantry to fetch some jam.' I entered the room and sat down at the long table. I looked at the jars. That was a *lot* of jam.

From the kitchen I looked out to the yard. A Volvo station wagon was parked close to the house. Dried mud came up to the windows. Behind it, there was another car. It had no wheels and was propped up on four piles of bricks.

The kitchen was spacious and light and full of stuff that didn't work any more and was going to be repaired or maybe had just been forgotten. There was a new stove next to the worktop, and in a corner stood a black wood burner, and the kitchen was warm and outside it was sunny, and light was everywhere. It was all very fine, but I had put my sunglasses on, just in case, and Signe didn't mention them when she served me four thick slices of home-made bread on a board and added butter and jam. I ate as if it were the last food in the world, and Signe said:

'There's more where that came from, so you just take it easy. Enjoy the food.' So I took it easy, and when I was almost finished, I heard heavy, shuffling footsteps in the hall. I stopped eating and looked up at the door. A big man was leaning against the door frame. He grinned at me. He had a stick in one hand and the other he was running through his close-cropped hair, and his hands were as big as boulders, and his bulging chest looked rock-hard.

'Well, there's the boy with the white bum,' he said. Slowly I stood up from the table, there was no other door into the room, and the window looked as if it hadn't been opened for years, and then I edged round the table and started to run towards him. It was like running into a brick wall. He *was* rock-hard. He let go of the stick and grabbed me round one shoulder, held my hair and looked me straight in the eye. He didn't blink, and his eyes were the brilliant blue of a child.

'Hello there, you young billy goat,' he smiled. 'What I meant to say was that if it hadn't been for your bum I would never have seen you. I was in the Volvo, and suddenly I saw something white by the river that wasn't there before, so of course I had to stop. You didn't look too clever, I can tell you.' He let go of my hair and stroked my cheek, and his hand was huge and dry and rough as the rock it resembled, and I stood quite still, and then I couldn't hold back, and I started to cry. The tears came from everywhere in floods, and he gently pushed me back into the kitchen.

'Eat up,' he said, 'and then come out to the cowshed and

we can have a chat. I could do with a hand. My legs are not what they used to be.'

I sat back down at the table and ate the last slice and cried into the jam and Signe stood humming with her back to me and bent down to put more wood into the black stove. The fire was rumbling, and finally I was both full and empty and bursting at the seams.

'When you've finished, you go out and find Leif, if you feel like it,' Signe said.

I walked out into the sunshine with my dark glasses on. I couldn't see Leif anywhere, but there was an old man in overalls standing in the yard. He was thin as a rake and tall, the overalls hung off his shoulders like a flabby tent, and he was holding his hands against the small of his back, gazing up into the air, so I too looked up, but there was nothing there, just air. Then he was aware of me, and he turned on his heel, and we stood up straight staring at each other, and he shook his head and stroked his chin and made a friendly gesture. I did the same, and when he smiled his face split in two, and he was off across the yard and behind the barn.

'That's Bjørn, the farm boy,' Signe said behind me. I turned and there she was, standing in the doorway with a swill bucket in her hand. 'He helps round here, looks after the horse and mucks out the cowshed. It's the last door on the right,' she said, pointing. I walked that way. The hook was off and the door was ajar, and through the crack I could hear Leif swearing like a trooper.

'Goddamnit, you're tryin' to teach your father to fuck?'
he yelled, and then I heard a bang. When I entered, it was
half dark, but past the empty stalls I could make him out
among a few calves. In each hand he had a shiny pail. The
biggest calf had small horns already and was banging
against the nearest pail, pulling and tugging at the tether
and making a hell of a row. Leif leaned over to put the pail
in the trough, and the calf jerked its head and hit him on
the temple.

'You bastard!' he shouted and dropped the pail on the
floor and smacked the calf between the eyes. It gave a jolt.
It's going to keel over, I thought, I was certain of it, for his
hands were like sledgehammers. But it shook its head and
beat a retreat. Leif turned, holding his forehead and
grinned.

'Rearing the young is a tricky business.'

'Is that what you do to children?' I said slowly, sensing
the open door behind me, and I already knew his legs were
bad. The place stank of cow muck and cow feed, and calf
bodies were crashing about in the murk, and he looked at
me with round eyes. Then he shook his head and said:

'People are not animals, Audun.' He bent over the calf
and patted its flank. I had no idea how he knew my name.
He pushed the pail over to the calf.

'You halfwit, Ferdinand, now there'll be less for you. It's
your own fault,' and the calf slurped up what was left in
the pail, and Leif gently rested his upper chest on Ferdinand's
back and stroked its flank, and the calf stood quite still and
just slurped. Leif straightened up, holding on to the calf's
back, grabbed his stick and came over to me.

'Ferdinand will be a good bull, but he'll be big, and it's just as well he learns who's boss from the off. Soon it will be too late.'

We walked out into the sun. I felt fine now. Apart from one thing.

'How did you know my name?' I said.

He laughed. 'It was written on the inside of your rucksack. Come on, let's go and say hello to Toughie.'

'Who's that?'

'The scourge of the chicken run.'

Toughie was a fox. He was tied up behind the barn and was almost tame, and wonderful to behold at close quarters. When Leif approached, Toughie jumped up on the leash and smiled as foxes do but he wasn't that tame. Whenever he screamed there was chaos in the chicken run. But no one would let Toughie go. They had grown to love him, and they would either have to kill him or drive him miles away, and that was not an option.

'A fox is a fox,' Leif said, 'and now that he knows his way around, it's no good to have him running loose.'

We walked around, and Leif showed me the place. The stable, the sheep shed, the tractor that wouldn't start just now, and the two baby goats he kept for entertainment.

'We've got no TV here, Audun, and we have to have something to amuse ourselves with.' And he pointed to the yellow barn and said: 'Isn't it fine,' and I said it was, and then we crossed the yard, and Leif got in behind the wheel of the Volvo, and I got in on the other side.

'I've a job for you,' he said. 'Let's drive off now, and if you see something on the road I should brake for, anything living or breathing or whatever, you tell me in good time.'

'Right,' I said. I didn't understand why, but we drove off, and for a minute there I was afraid we were going back the way I had come, but we didn't. We were going to the shop and that was in the opposite direction. At one point I saw a tractor ahead of us on the road, and I told Leif in good time, and then he put his right hand under his right leg and lifted it off the accelerator and on to the brake, and we stopped just a metre from it.

'Leg's not what it used to be,' Leif said.

I was there for a whole week. At night I slept in the room beneath the skylight, and in the morning I got up, and Signe served me her home-made bread in the kitchen. And then I worked most of the day on the jobs that Leif decided I could manage. There were more and more, and I could not get enough, and in the evening I swam in the river at a far better spot than the first one I found. At ten o'clock I was sent upstairs with a hug from Signe, and I was so greedy for it that I blushed. I tried to think as little as possible, I just drank it all in. On Wednesday one of their sons came up and fixed the tractor. They let me join him for a test drive, and then I drove it alone across the farmyard with everyone watching and cheering. The engine roared, and I sat up high, and I could steer it wherever I wanted to go.

On Saturday it was raining, and Leif said 'Thank God,

that's not a day too soon', and for the first time, I went out into the yard without my sunglasses on.

When I got up on the eighth day and went downstairs, my father was standing in the kitchen. He was smiling, and he was clean-shaven, but in his eyes I could see what was in store for me. Leif was sitting at the table looking down as I came in.

'Sorry, Audun, but I couldn't bring myself to tell you. We had to let them know. Anything else would be illegal.'

IV

13

I rein myself in. On the first day I take the Metro from Veitvet, get off just a few stations closer to Oslo and cross under a railway bridge where I can see the sky between the sleepers above my head, and I walk up a road with factory buildings and warehouses lined up on each side, until I am at the top. Behind a warehouse storing washing powder and down another road to the left, I see the tall, grey Alles Hjem office block across the way, with a car park on the opposite side. The production plant is behind the office block. You cannot see it from the road. I try the main door I entered last week, but it is locked and dark inside. I rattle the brass handle until I realise the people up above don't start until half-past eight. Now it's only half-past six, and I walk around the building and find a small gate and enter the yard where there is a loading ramp the entire length of the wall. Pallets are stacked up in rows with waste paper compressed into bales, and I walk along the ramp and in through the plastic flap doors where the forklifts come and go.

The large room I walk into is the finishing shop. Just inside the door there are pallets of shrink-wrapped maga-zines shoulder to shoulder, twenty-five in each rack, and twelve racks high, ready for the distribution centre, and right in front the conveyors, long and low, and one so new you can still see the blue paint. Last week when I was here with the foreman, waiting to be shown round, a little man came down from his platform. His forearms were as big as Popeye's, and he grabbed my shoulders in an iron grip.

'Are you going to work here?' he said.

'I think so.'

'Don't,' he said, pulling me away to his station on the conveyor. 'Look. Do you know how long I've been working here? I've been working here for fifteen years, and in all those years I've been standing in front of this box, stuffing printed matter into that hole, and do you know what?'

'No.'

'It never gets full.'

'Doesn't it?'

'Do you understand what I'm saying? It never gets full!' He held me round the shoulders so tight, it was hard to say anything but:

'Let go for fuck's sake.' Luckily the foreman came up, and the man let go of me, and we moved on.

'You won't be working here,' he said. 'You'll be working on the rotary press.'

'Fine,' I said.

'Don't mind him. He's a philosopher.'

'Right.'

The rotary press is at the other end of the hall and down the stairs. I walk slowly down the two landings to the clocking-in machine. I find my card and stick it in the slot and the sound makes me jump. The ink is black – one minute past seven it is red – and then I enter the cloakroom.

All the mirrors, all the basins with the *No washing feet or clothes* signs, the ugly yellow walls just like they were at Rosenhoff School, the grey metal cabinets one after the other, old men and young bikers, suddenly like big birds with their shirt tails flapping over bare thighs and white calves and then all in their blue work gear. Confident, seasoned.

I hate the thought of flapping my wings among them and try to delay it, but in the end I have to, and when I have finished, the new work clothes with their sharp creases are stiff and dark blue compared to the lighter, faded blue of the others. Behind me someone is whistling a wedding march, and I itch all over. I head for the door.

The concourse is strange and quiet and not as I remember it from my guided tour. The printing presses just *stand* there, three floors high, not a grain of dust stirring, and the air is cold against my face. I walk past the Number Three and on through a large door to the next concourse where only one press is standing, but this one is even bigger. Here is where I am going to work. At this machine. Seven men sit in two separate groups: printers and assistants. I am the one they're waiting for, and when I enter, they all look towards the door, and a frighteningly tall, powerful man stands up and goes towards the console. I haven't said hello to any of them, and I think maybe I should, but nobody seems to expect anything of the kind and I stand out on the floor between the two groups like an idiot with my arms hanging down like a pair of wooden planks. The tall man turns and yells:

'TROND!'

'Yes!' someone tries to yell back, but his voice cracks at the top.

'You tell this new . . . what's your name?' he shouts to me.

'Audun Sletten,' I say. My voice sounds reedy.

'You explain to this Letten what his job is!' Goliath shouts to the one called Trond. 'He's on C press.'

'Sletten!' I shout. Everyone looks at me and grins.

'What?'

'My name is Sletten, not LETTEN!' I yell and feel my face itching. There is an echo in the room, and Letten bounces around like a ping-pong ball up under the ceiling.

'Oh my God, did I get it wrong?' Goliath says with a smirk. 'It's these ear protectors. They're no good. My hearing's damaged.'

Blood's pounding in my ears, sweat running down my back. I clench my fists and raise them slowly, but no one even looks at me. I can hear their mocking laughter, and then they all get up and walk towards the press, and they are all bigger than me, and they laugh and shake their heads.

'That was some entrance you made,' Trond says, coming over to show me what they call C press.

'Very funny,' I say.

Trond is lanky and thin, has a Keith Richards haircut and a ring in his left ear and close up, he seems pretty normal.

'What do you think of the Stones?' he asks.

'They're OK,' I say, 'but Hendrix is better.'

'Jimi Hendrix is a Negro, for Christ's sake. And he's dead, isn't he?'

'That's true, but without the Negroes the Stones would have played the tuba. And that's a fact.'

'Hendrix is OK,' Trond says, 'but myself, I prefer the Stones.'

'So I can see,' I say, and Trond grins.

Goliath starts the press on slow, there is a jerk and everything begins to roll slowly.

'All right,' Trond says, 'in front of you there are four drums, one on top of the other. Above and below them there are the ink rollers. The ink is pumped from the barrels. The printing plates are attached to the top and bottom drums, the two in the middle have rubber blankets. The ink rollers rotate against the plates, the plates against the rubber and the rubber against the paper. On the back of the paper web, there's a huge steel cylinder that the paper wraps around. You can't see it now, but it weighs so many bloody tons you can't even imagine. If anything goes wrong when it's moving, all hell will break loose.'

'Right,' I say.

'Right,' Trond says. 'When we start up, no old ink on the rubber, it will clog, and then the blankets split, and the print is ruined, and every time we start up, the blankets have to be soaking wet or else the paper gets stuck to the ink when the plates slam on, and then it rips, and we have to spend hours with tweezers getting off all the stuff that's got stuck. It's a crap job. When I say wet, I mean wet, but not with water. White spirit. There's a bucket on the stand behind you. Right?'

'Right.'

'You must never use water, spit, cry or piss on the paper.

It can't take it, it rips straight away, and we have to re-thread the whole paper web. We do that as little as possible. It's really boring work and nobody gets a break. When you wash the blankets, you use rubber gloves and those rags there, under the bucket stand. If you don't, your skin will go red and after a couple of weeks it starts to fall off. Right?'

'Right,' I say.

'If you feel the rag being pulled from your hands, never do the first thing that occurs to you.'

'No? And what's the first thing that occurs to me?'

'Holding on to it. What happens then, we call losing your maidenhead. It often happens to new people. So let go and stop the press. The red button is there on your left. Right?'

'Right,' I say, and worry a little about that maidenhead thing, but I don't want to ask. I make a mental note of the red button.

'OK, wash away.' And I wash. I'm clumsy and nervous and hold the rag too tight, wondering where my maidenhead is. It takes some time, it's like the ink is glued on, but then most of it is gone, and the blankets are wet, and Trond yells:

'READY!' And suddenly it's like standing on the runway at Gardermoen airport as a jumbo jet takes off. The press shrieks and howls and BANG! BANG! go the drums as they hit the cylinder, and the roar gets louder as the speed increases. I cover my ears. Trond looks at me and grins, points his finger to his temple and turns it. OK, there is something I don't know, and now he will tell me. Trond steps behind the press and comes back with two small boxes. He gives one to me, and inside are two yellow foam rubber thingies.

'Watch. Like this!' he shouts in my ear and rolls the thingies between his fingers until they are small and narrow, and then he stuffs them in his ears. I do the same with mine. The roar subsides, the foam rubber expands, it's a strange and slightly awkward feeling, the noise becomes distant, and it's a little like being high. If anyone tapped me on the head, there would be an echo.

Trond shouts again.

'WHAT?'

'You'll have to learn sign language! It's a hundred decibels in here!'

Inside the soundproof room we remove the earplugs, and even though it's supposed to be quiet in here, all sounds seem sharper than before. My first thought is to put the plugs back in.

'In six months you'll have ear canals like a cow's arse,' Trond says. 'This being your debut, Samuel will be first on the stacker and then me. But don't wander off. If the paper tears, and you're not here, you'll have Long John on your back.'

Long John: that would be Goliath. Goliath suits him better, but I guess I'll keep that to myself. I am not ready to play David.

14

Bᴀɴɢ!

I jump up from my post at the stacker, and I am up on the gallery within seconds. The paper has torn for the fifth time today and it's not yet ten o'clock. The whole time it's a hassle, I charge up the stairs like a madman to get there before the whole shebang catches fire. Something is not right. Each time the machine stops, the paper starts to burn.

The heat from the gas burners hits me as I run along the gallery and fling the small doors open. On my forearms, the few hairs I have left curl like tiny worms. I have been fast, but not fast enough. The flames lick out at the end of the top heater, and I rip the fire extinguisher off its stand and blast away, and films I have seen roll through my head, disaster films with flames out of control devouring everything, and here I stand with my three-litre extinguisher! If the machine oil catches fire, I'm done for.

The flames don't go out, they spread, and soon the paper web is ablaze. I am so tired I am burning, my chest is hot and my back is freezing, and I run along the gallery and around the machine and grab the second extinguisher and stand there alone between ceiling and floor in the large concourse shooting from the hip like some crazed Western hero.

'SAMUEL!' I yell. Jesus, I'm new here, why don't they help? Then I see it: it's the gas in the burners, they're not switched off. It's supposed to cut off automatically when the machine stops, but there is a blue hiss in there. No wonder it's on fire.

'SAMUEL! FOR FUCK'S SAKE, SWITCH THE GAS OFF!'

Samuel is sitting inside the soundproof room. I can see him when I bend down: he is smoking and reading an old *Playboy*, or looking at the pictures, that is, because he can't read English. My voice must have cut through. He gets up from his chair, puts the magazine down and grinds out the cigarette with a steel-toed shoe. I have thought about it many times: why does he wear those protective shoes? The heaviest thing he has ever dropped on them is a pack of cigarettes. He goes over to the console and switches the gas off, steps back to his chair and lights another cigarette, opens *Playboy*, and he doesn't even send me a glance. I stand up, there is the taste of ash in my mouth. I lick my lips, but it won't go away.

In fact, we have the same job. Assistant rotary press operator, it says in the files. But as I am thirty years younger than him and new to the job, Samuel has awarded himself an age increment, which means that every time something happens, he stays in his chair, while I rush around like a maniac.

Of course, there are Trond and Jan, but Jan is off sick, and Trond is on the toilet and has been there for a long time. Trond is the ballet dancer of the workplace, he finds his way everywhere, he can turn his hand to *everything*, he is full of humour as dry as the air we work in and has a knack of being on the toilet each time the paper tears.

I slide down the banister from the gallery and cut the paper just before the fire reaches the one-ton heavy roll, and then I race back up again. With the gas switched off it's easy to control the flames. I pull out the rest of the paper, sweep up a hundred metres of red-hot web and stuff the whole lot into the container for inflammable litter.

I brush the soot off my overalls. My forearms feel as dry as old cardboard, I am so tired, I am sweating and freezing, and I sit down on the lowest step of the stairs and roll a cigarette. To thread a new web alone is impossible.

Maggi walks past in a light blue coat with a notepad in her hand. She is forty-five years old, newly divorced and always cheerful.

'Goodness me, are you here on your own?' she says.

I do not answer, and she asks:

'Anything you need from the shop?' and stands with her pencil at the ready. Her job is to run errands, fill the coffee machine and make everybody happy.

'Petterøe 3 and rolling paper. Rizla.' She writes it down as she is leaving and waves over her shoulder and is gone. With numb fingers, I roll the shreds of tobacco I have left. The cigarette looks more like a trumpet, but I light up, and my hands are shaking, and then the foreman enters the room. His coat is spotless white, and he stops in front of me, looking at his watch as though it were some kind of new invention.

'Tell me something, Sletten, haven't you been here long enough to know the break starts at eleven and not at ten?'

I get to my feet, drop the cigarette and stub it out with my shoe.

'And I don't know if you've noticed, but there are some very serviceable ashtrays placed here and there on this floor.' He turns on his heel and brushes invisible dust off his coat. There is a bald patch at the back of his head, and his hand automatically shoots up to cover it, and then he is off through the doors at the far end of the hall. The doors slam shut, and the sound slams through my head, and there's a humming in there, for this is my father leaving, the way I saw him the last time he was home five years ago. It was Sunday morning, and we hadn't seen him for two weeks, and suddenly the door opens, and in he comes wearing the same clothes he wore when he left.

'Hello,' I say. I feel timid, but he doesn't answer anyway, just walks right past me to the stairs, his eyes fixed straight ahead, and then there is the smell of him, the smell of his jacket, his body, the smell of bonfire and forest and long-forgotten sunny Sundays, only so strong and unfamiliar in here. He hasn't shaved since he was last at home, maybe hasn't washed, either, and there are grey streaks in his beard I didn't know were there. I turn, and my mother is standing in the living room doorway, she doesn't speak, just gazes up the stairs, and I gaze up the stairs. We can hear him in the bedroom, he is taking his rucksack from the cupboard, pulls out the drawer of the bedside table, and we know what he's got there, the police never found it, and there is a clunk as he drops it into the rucksack. My mother mumbles something I can't make out, and upstairs he stuffs more things into the rucksack, and then he comes back down. I hold my breath, I do not breathe, my mother does not breathe, and he is outside, slamming the door behind him, and it slams through my head, and he didn't even look at me.

I run into the living room and across to the window and watch him walk down the gravel path to the gate. By the road, he stops and turns, puts his hand in the rucksack, pulls out the pistol and takes a shot at the house. There is the sound of thunder and lightning, and the bullet smashes through the kitchen window and hits the cupboard above the sink and bores a hole in the wall behind it, which is nothing but plasterboard, and maybe it goes right through to the living room. We stop at the kitchen threshold and dare not go any further. We can see the hole in the pane and we turn and look at the cupboard. There were three jars of strawberry jam on the middle shelf inside, and soon it is dripping red into the sink. Dripping and dripping, and then it starts to flow, but neither of us can make the effort to go in and open the cupboard door to see what's behind.

'My God, what shall I do?' my mother whispers. I close my eyes and see my father's hand raising the gun, there is a flash of light, for it is sunny outside, and I run back to the living room, the hall smelling of bonfire and forest and long-forgotten sunny Sundays, but when I look out the window, there is no one by the gate.

The next day my mother starts packing.

I look around for Samuel and catch sight of him half hidden behind the press where he is padding about with a broom, sweeping the ashes off the floor. As soon as the foreman's

146

through the door and gone, he drops the broom and goes into the soundproof room.

Trond comes whistling in where the foreman went out, he has a copy of *Melody Maker* tucked under his arm. He looks at me and grins.

'Tell me something, Sletten,' he says in a bossy voice. 'Are you sure the printing trade is right for you? Have you considered the Oslo Fire Brigade? Hell, can't I go to the shithouse for two minutes without you razing the whole place?' I don't answer. In a couple of months I might; for now, I just shrug.

'Samuel!' Trond shouts. 'Come on, we have to thread the paper.' To me he says, 'The printers are in the storeroom playing poker, so we'll have to do without them.'

We start the machine on slow, make a new cut in the paper and start threading it through the press, one man each side, round hundreds of cylinders and rollers. It takes ages, but everything runs smoothly, we could have done it with our eyes closed. When we've finished, we wash down the rubber blankets and have a smoke. We're not allowed to start up without the printers, so we just have to wait for Goliath and Elk to show up. But they don't, and Trond checks his watch.

'Lunchtime,' he says.

To get to the cloakroom, we have to go through the next concourse. I open the large door and walk straight into a wall of sound. The roar bounces off the walls and the compressed air valves make smacking sounds as the pressure is released, there is a loud whistle, the machines are coming in to land, everything moves, there is someone running, and the machines stop and go silent. A man I cannot see lets out a naked laugh, another man throws his lunch pack like a baseball, it fizzes in an arc through the air, and I can't resist, I jump and catch it in mid-flight and toss it into the nearest waste bin.

I hear 'Fuck you,' and there is a tingle in my spine, but I just put my hands up and move on without looking back.

In the canteen we help ourselves to coffee from the counter, find a table by the wall, and Trond pulls a pack of cards from his pocket and starts to shuffle. We are the first ones here, it's perfectly still, and we hear the clatter from the kitchen and the canteen lady humming. Trond deals with practised fingers, five cards each, and the door opens and all the others come streaming in wearing blue, ink-stained work clothes, and their hands are flushed from the white spirit and strong soap. They are shouting and laughing about something that has happened, but we don't know what that is, and we don't care. But when everyone has sat down, Jonny comes bursting in, five hours late today with his hair standing on end, and his face as red as his hands. He isn't close enough for me to smell him, but I know he reeks of alcohol. He pours himself a large mug of coffee and chuckles at something only he knows about. On his way from the counter, he stops at the window facing the car park and looks out.

'I'll be damned,' he says. 'Did I come in the car today?'

Everyone cracks up laughing, they slap their thighs and roar with laughter, but I can see from Jonny's face that he is not joking, he is staring in disbelief at the yellow Opel Kadett parked crosswise out there. His eyes are rimmed with white as he runs the gauntlet through the canteen and sits down at a table by himself. He lowers his head, and I pick up my cards, but I don't look at them, I look at Jonny and think back to the first time I saw him, charging from the gallery of Number Three with a test print in his hand. Everything was wrong, no one was doing their job, and he was so furious the blue veins on his forehead stood out, and on his back there were big patches of sweat, and he scurried in between the machinery and started to dance along the ink regulators, twisting them like a lunatic, and then he was out again and off to the paper-folder for another test. Kneeling down, with a magnifying glass in his hand, pirouetting up, waving the print in the air he smacked it down on the table and said:

'This is how it should look, this is pro work, damnit!' And I guess he's right, that's what pro work looks like, but now he is empty, and I know he is finished. He'll get the boot for certain, he'll keep drinking until he ends up under the bridges along the Aker river or standing at the soup kitchen with his hand stretched out, his gaze turned in, saying:

'Got any change, pal?' And then he'll die thirty years before his time.

There is a downward pull in the space around him, like at the edge of a cliff where half of you wants to jump and the rest of you holds back, and it makes me furious, makes me want to lash out. I can't concentrate, and I chuck my cards on the table.

'What's up with you?' Trond asks, impatient. 'Why can't you sit still like other people do?' But I cannot and I get up, and there he is, the guy with the lunch pack. He started working here a month before me and is a veteran and doesn't like me taking liberties.

'Leaving, are you, tough guy?' he says. I feel the heat rising. There's no avoiding this, and he could not have chosen a better time. I round the table and face him and say:

'No, I was going to come and see if you had any food left, I'm so goddamn hungry today.' I haven't said anything so stupid for years, but now he is forced to do something and shoves me hard in the chest. I would have toppled over without the table behind me. It's a long time since I've been in a situation like this, but I made up my mind years ago that, if I ever were, I would be ready, and I lash out at once. The pain that shoots up my arm is so fierce that the first thing I think of is how much it must have hurt him, because I hit him right under the eye. He howls and crashes backwards, and I hold my arm, it hurts so much I could scream. I take two deep breaths, and then there is a racket in the canteen, and someone grabs me from behind and lifts me off my feet. I kick out and the someone hisses in my ear:

'You fucking idiot, you're not even through your probation period yet!' It's Goliath: he carries me through the canteen to the door and lobs me into the corridor without drawing an extra breath, I could have been his teddy bear, if he ever had such a thing. My knee smashes against the opposite wall. There is something expanding in my chest like a balloon, it's swelling and pushing from the inside, it makes me dizzy, and I jump up and hurl myself at him and throw a left hook into his stomach. It's a wonderful feeling, I have felt like doing it for weeks. A strange noise comes from his mouth, but then I feel a smack above my ear, and I am on the floor. There is a rushing sound and then a howl in my ear, and I can barely hear what he says:

'If I were you, I would clear off and get down behind the machine until this blows over. You and I can settle up some other time. You goddamn squirt!' He slams the door, and the bang bounces through my skull, and the corridor goes quiet. The only noise is in my ear. I limp to the stairs. My knee hurts, and I have to take the steps sideways, it is three floors down to the print shop, and I try not to think. I haven't really seen this staircase before. It is painted yellow, and I cling to that. But of course, that's not a whole lot.

On the ground floor I meet Maggi. She comes from the lift with her trolley on her way back from the shop. She stops.

'Here's your tobacco,' she says. 'That's twenty-five kroner.'

'What tobacco?'

'You ordered a pack of tobacco. Have you gone senile?'

'I'm not senile. It's my head. It hurts.' I try to put my hand in my pocket for money, but my arm is paralysed.

'Let me,' she says and thrusts her hand into my pocket, rummaging around and fiddling with all kinds of things, I gasp, and she winks, finds the money and counts off what I owe her and stuffs the rest back with a broad beam. And then, in a friendly way, she pats me hard on the knee.

'Ouch!' I scream. She laughs, loud and husky, wags her finger and goes into the finishing shop.

In the cloakroom I sit on the bench in front of my cabinet, stick my bad hand under my shirt and rub my knee with the other. It's strange when there's no one here, very unfamiliar and quiet, just grey and a hideous yellow, wet patches under the sinks, and I try to remember why I quit school. I don't remember anything, and I sit there for a long time, my mind a blank, until I hear sounds that might be laughter on the stairs. It gets louder, and I hear the steel-toed shoes on the floor, but still no one has opened the door. I get up and stare at the door and wait, thinking maybe Trond was right. Maybe the printing business is not the trade for me.

15

Kjartan, called Elk because of his size and his gait, approaches A press waving a spatula knife in his right hand. Elk is the deputy printer and fifty-three years old, he is recently and unhappily divorced and has a mass of grey hair above his heavy face. I stand by the stacker, handing out sixteen-page sheets on a vibration plate, working them and piling them 32 high on a pallet. Soon I will have been here for two months, and no one can complain about my skills, the printed sheets go on the pallet in razor-sharp stacks. There are 12,500 sheets on each pallet, that is 25 sheets per stack and this is the tenth pallet today. For once we haven't had a single paper break, and I am exhausted by the everlasting thunder of the press. It gets into your bones and in the end turns them into jelly.

I follow Elk out of the corner of my eye. I have just reported a blemish on the print. For the moment it's outside the cut, but it is growing and soon it will be on the printed page itself. It has to be a build-up of ink on the rubber blanket. I reported it only because I am dying for a fag and know we will have to stop the press to remove it. I stand there shifting my feet, my pack of Petterøe out and ready, and I am just waiting for Elk to give the stop signal to Goliath, who is the head printer.

The spatula is gleaming. I was the one who cleaned it,

it's part of the job. Assistants clean the printers' tools. It's ridiculous, they could do it for themselves. But they insist, they want to maintain the line of command.

Elk paces around the machine. He closes one eye as if taking aim, a strange sight that is, and then he goes down on one knee, holds the spatula at an angle to the whirling rubber blanket, supports his arm with his left hand, and I realise he is not going to stop the press. The cylinders are rotating at 18,000 revolutions per hour: all you see is the newsprint flashing by. Goliath is in the cage behind the console reading a tabloid. No one else in sight.

From the large windows up under the ceiling a ray of sun comes shining into the concourse, so powerful and tangible you could bang your head on it, if that's what you wanted to do. All of a sudden there are sparks raining through the room making the sun seem like a torch with a flat battery. Something flies through the air, and I feel a smarting pain in my earlobe. Christ, I could have been killed. A chill runs down my spine. I go numb, completely rigid, my brain slams the brakes on and comes to a stand-still. And then I see the jet of blood. I start to run, I throw myself at the red button, so far from my post at the stacker, and the sound of the machine coming to a halt is like a plane crashing. Suddenly I realise Elk is drunk, that he smelt of alcohol when I reported the blemish.

'We'll fix that,' he said with a crooked grin, and that was the first time I'd ever seen him smile. Now the great Elk is standing with one hand bleeding, screaming:

'MY FINGERS, OH FUCK, I GOTTA FIND MY FINGERS!'

There are three fingers missing from his left hand. Goliath comes running in, he tries to calm Elk down, he has a rag he wants to wrap round the injured hand. He gulps so hard you can really see it, and he holds Elk tight around the shoulder, but Elk, who is almost as tall and even stronger, tears himself away and starts running in circles.

'FUCK FUCK OH FUCK I GOTTA FIND MY FINGERS!'

People rush in from all sides and crowd around the A press, and we look for Elk's fingers, but they are nowhere to be found, and to be honest, I'd prefer not to find them.

Goliath tries to catch the eye of the man with the large face that is the same colour now as his hair, and his hand just bleeds and bleeds.

'Hello Kjartan . . . Kjartan.' For once Goliath speaks gently. 'Hello, Kjartan, take it easy now. Let's get out of here. I'll drive you to casualty. Come on now, Kjartan!'

Elk stares at Goliath with a strange, distant look in his eyes and then he shouts: 'BUT DON'T YOU GET IT I HAVE TO FIND MY FUCKING FINGERS THEY HAVE TO BE SEWN BACK ON!'

But we can't find his fingers, and Goliath forces Elk to go with him. He has lost so much blood that his knees are giving way, and he doesn't look so tall any more. On their way out, they pass the foreman, who looks around him. Goliath doesn't even turn his head, and as I am the one standing closest to the foreman, he asks me:

'What's going on here?'

'Kjartan's lost three fingers.'

'Oh. Jesus!' The manager sees all the blood and says Jesus again. Then he looks at me.

'What happened to you? Your ear is bleeding.' I touch my earlobe, and there is blood on my fingers.

'The spatula knife,' I say.

'The spatula?' Then it dawns on him. 'So where the hell were you standing?'

'By the stacker.' Everyone looks back at the belt. In the wall behind the half-filled pallet is Elk's spatula knife, centimetres into the plaster.

'Oh, Jesus,' the foreman says. 'You could have had your skull sliced in two!' He runs his hand through the hair he has left and leaves the concourse smoking nervously and goes up to the office where he spends most of the day flicking through pornographic magazines.

We wash off the blood, remove the ripped rubber blanket and stretch a new one around the drum, and we can go home.

In the cloakroom, the ever-hip Trond says: 'At least I'm no longer the only one here with a pierced ear.'

The next day Trond calls me over. He is behind the press cleaning up. We have finished the print run and have to wash everything down before we start afresh.

'Just look there,' he says.

In the water tank, Elk's fingers are floating. They are swollen and look like big snails. I throw up straight into the tank. The foreman, who is doing his inspection tour has recovered well from yesterday's ordeal and says:

'You'll have to clean that up yourself, Sletten!' And I have to wash the tank and remove my vomit and Elk's three fingers.

'I don't want to watch this,' Trond says, making himself scarce. I don't really know what to do with the fingers. In the end I wrap them in some waste paper and throw them in the rubbish container. And then I go to the toilet and throw up once more.

It's dark on my way home from the late shift. No one lives in this area. Along the road down to the Metro station there are nothing but factories and warehouses, and in a few offices the lights are still on. The old street lamps are hanging on rotting posts and swing in the wind and creak in their rusting metal holders, and most of them are smashed anyway. I am walking alone. There is no one else going my way that I feel like talking to. Trond lives in Lørenskog, and he has a car and all, and besides, I have fallen out with plenty of people.

The early winter gloom devours everything. Litter blows down the gravel road, through the grey I can see the white of it rolling along the ditches, and it's so quiet I can hear the rustle and the echo of my footsteps. Beneath the railway bridge it is totally dark, but then I see the lights from the Metro station, so I walk the last stretch a little faster. I pay at the barrier where a sleepy ticket collector sits reading the magazine I work on every day. He could have saved himself the trouble, it won't make him any smarter. Down the steps I can hear my heart beating.

The train arrives on schedule. Inside the carriage I try to read, but I am tired, and before I am even able to concentrate, I see Linderud station disappearing behind me, so I just have to put the book in my bag.

I am the only person to get off at Veitvet. There is a hollow echo between the concrete walls on my way down the stairs, and another sleepy ticket collector is sitting at the barrier reading the same magazine. Perhaps Oslo Transport Company buys up remaindered copies, hell, I don't know, but I am about to drop a remark. I decide not to. It's half-past eleven, and my whole body is aching. When I close my eyes, I can see the fingers in the tank.

I go out through the glass door by the Narvesen kiosk, and as I'm about to start down the steps to Veitvetveien, someone behind me shouts softly.

'Hi, Audun!' I turn. And there are Dole and Willy plus two others. Dole is smiling. I am a dead man. Quickly and quietly they spread out: they know how to do this, they have seen it in films, and there is no point trying to escape. I rest the bag against the railings. This is the moment I have to rise out of myself and become someone else: Martin Eden or Jean-Paul Belmondo or Albert Finney in *Saturday Night and Sunday Morning*. I too have seen the films. It will be all right. Arvid and I used to talk about it, it's the only way to keep your dignity. Or else they own you. I smile at Dole and splay my hands.

'Out late?' I say. He smiles back, There's one thing we both know: I am finished. And then the film unravels. A man in dark clothes comes skulking along the walls from the shopping centre. Geir's bar has just closed, and he is not too steady on his feet, but still he can probably make it wherever he wants to go. I don't know if it's him, his face is shrouded in the darkness by the station, and I am not used to seeing him here among the houses and streets and shopping centres, but it looks like his walk, and as he slips by, I say to Dole:

'Just wait a moment!' and take a few steps after the man and shout: 'Hey, you! Stop,' although I am not really sure I want him to stop. But anyway, he doesn't stop. I am about to run after him, and his back melts into the shadows up towards Trondhjemsveien and the woods on the other side, and Dole leaps out and blocks my way.

'That was a new one,' he says, 'but it won't fuckin' work, Audun, you're goin' nowhere.' And then he lashes out. I am not prepared for it, my guard isn't up yet, and he hits me in the mouth. I am about to shout 'Wait!' but it hurts so much the word doesn't reach my lips, and they are all over me, the four of them, punching and kicking, and I get my beating, with no dignity, Martin Eden and Albert Finney are over the hills and long gone. Finally, I am on the asphalt and all I can do is protect my face. Dole gives me a last kick and says:

'Goodnight, Audun,' and clatters down the stairs with the others. I hear Willy's laughter, and then they are gone.

I am not sure I'm able to stand up. There is a smell of dust and beer and tarmac. I lick my lips. I can't feel my mouth, but it tastes of blood. It hurts to breathe, I cough and the pain shoots across my ribcage. Dole's last kick was vicious.

I lift myself up, I can just about do it, my arms stiff and sore, and finally I get on my feet. Straight ahead is the sign for the bowling alley. It's dark inside, but the sign is luminous. I look towards the stairs. There is my bag. I walk slowly over and pick it up. It's painful. I can hardly bend down. I look around. Everything is quiet by the Metro. If anyone saw what happened, they have legged it. I look in through the station windows. The ticket collector is hunched over a crossword. He is deaf and blind. How he can even see that crossword is beyond me. He can go to hell.

I can't go home like this. My mother will be hysterical and start fussing and ask me all kinds of questions. I don't think I can face it. I hold the bag close to my chest and spit. There is a red spot on the asphalt. I put my hand to my mouth, and I can feel how my upper lip is split. I need help for this. Very slowly I walk round the shopping centre, past the rear entrance to Geir's bar and down past the youth club and the post office. If I keep my back straight, my chest doesn't hurt so much.

'Anything comes up, you know where I live,' old Abrahamsen said. He lives at the far end of Veitvetsvingen in a three-room terraced house. I take him at his word. I don't know where else to go. I could go to Arvid's, but I have hardly seen him the last month, and I would feel awkward.

I come to the bend in the road. There are cars parked the whole way down. People have more cars than they used to. I cough as gently as I can and ring the bell of the last house. When the bell stops ringing, it is dead quiet. I turn to see if anyone is standing there gawping, but there is no one about. I have two holes in my trousers, one on each knee, and there's only one button left on my jacket. A noise comes from behind the door, and then it opens and old Abrahamsen peers out. He's in his underwear. Of course he is, it's late. I check my watch, but it's broken and stopped at ten to twelve.

'I'll be damned, it's that boy.' He smiles. I try to smile back, but I cannot: moving my lips hurts too much. He opens the door and the light streams out from the hall. I close my eyes.

'For fuck's sake, Audun, what's this you look like? Get yourself in here.' I squint and try, but I can't move my left leg up his steps. It has gone all stiff. He comes outside and supports my arm, and I limp indoors. I have never been to his place before. I had pictured an old man's flat with an oilcloth on the table, elks in the sunset, discoloured wall lamps and unwashed, brown coffee mugs. But the walls are freshly painted and covered with framed pictures and photographs and the kitchen is spotless. In the living room there are several paintings and two bookshelves, and there is a zebra skin hanging on the longest wall. There is not one picture of anything in Norway. He sees what I am looking at and says:

'I was a seaman. You didn't know, did you? Can you manage to take your clothes off?' I nod. I can if I have to.

'You need to take a shower to see what's what.' I nod again and start to undress. The jacket and the shirt I can do, but I can't do the trousers, it feels like my ribs crack when I bend down. I look at him and shrug and shake my head.

'If it's fine with you, I can do it,' he says, and I nod. It's fine with me. And old Abrahamsen kneels down and pulls off my jeans and boots. His hair has gone grey, but it's all there, the sinewy arms in the vest work at my laces, he is quick and his muscles ripple, it looks good, and I think: to look like that when you're past sixty.

He pushes me gently towards the bathroom. I stop him, I want to tell him something, but it's too difficult, it turns to mush in my mouth, and I make a sign with my hand. He goes to fetch paper and a pencil. I write: 'Could you please call my mother and tell her not to worry?'And I add the telephone number.

'I'll sort that out, Audun. You take that shower.'

I do. The water is lukewarm and pleasant. It runs red down my stomach and on to the white, painted cement floor, like a rusty snake coiling, and then tapers down the drain. Carefully I dry myself and look into the mirror. Jesus Christ.

He knocks on the door and comes in with plasters and iodine in a little bottle. He stands watching me, shaking his head.

'How do you feel?' he says.

'It hurts.'

'A lot?'

I nod. He opens the bottle, cleans the wounds with some cotton wool and puts on the plasters. I stand quite still with my eyes closed. Once, by mistake, his elbow touches my ribs. I groan. He presses his finger softly in a few places. I groan again.

'A couple of broken ribs would be my guess,' he says, 'it hurts, but it's no disaster. Well, this is as much as I can do.

162

I'm not sure about your lip, though. You'll need to go to casualty with that.' He tilts his head and smiles.

'I remember one time I looked a bit like you do now. I was about your age too. It was in Hull, that was, a few years after the First World War. I had signed on a freight vessel. A Dane beat me up, I didn't stand a chance. He was two metres of muscle from Hirtshals. We became friends later on. We'd had a pint too many, that's all. You know, I could tell you some things about Hull. It was a great place. Not many people liked it, but I did. And here's me telling stories. You need some clothes.'

He goes out and rummages around in a wardrobe and returns with a worn, grey suit, measures me up with one eye pinched and helps me on with the trousers. The suit fits and feels good. It's clean.

'That's it, you have to look presentable in casualty, other-wise they won't treat you properly.' He rings for a taxi and puts on a jumper, jacket and shoes. He is going with me.

In the taxi down Trondhjemsveien, I huddle in the corner of the back seat. I feel better now, the engine hums and ticks over like a taxi should. I could have gone to sleep had it not been for my aching mouth and chest. I close my eyes and then old Abrahamsen says:

'I don't have to tell you, Audun, you know for yourself. You're eighteen years old. It's a tricky time. There's so much going on, and later some say it was the best time they ever had, and some say it was the worst, and they're both right. People live different lives. People *are* different. Some get the cream, always, oh, I've seen them. But one thing is certain: at some point everything changes. You're not

eighteen all your life. That may not be much of a consola-
tion, but take a hint from someone who's on the outside
looking in: you'll get through this. I'm dead sure.'

The doctor is tired and irritable. The first thing he says:
    'Is this your doing?' looking old Abrahamsen in the eye.
    'Thanks for the compliment. Could I have done all that
to such a strong fellow without a single scratch in return?
Thank you very much!' He bows, and the doctor is even
more irritable. He tells me to get on the table, where I lie
flat and he shines a lamp in my face and leans over me.
There are black rings under his eyes and he needs a shave.
    'Right,' he says, 'you have a choice. I can either stitch
you up without an anaesthetic and it will heal just fine, or
you can have an injection, and you'll look into the mirror
three weeks from now wondering where you got the hare
lip.' He talks like James Cagney, if Cagney had spoken
Norwegian, there is a touch of American movie about the
room, and it isn't much of a choice.
    'No anaethedic,' I say.
    When he has finished he puts a big plaster over the cut,
giving me a snub nose, he winds a bandage round my chest,
and to his back I say 'Thank you very much'.
    'OK, next,' he shouts through the door, and we go down
the corridor, past reception and on through the double
doors to the square in front and look for a taxi. I am dizzy
with fatigue and pain, and in the car I say the only right
thing.
    'Tell me bou Hull.'

164

Old Abrahamsen smiles and tells me about Hull. About sailing down the Humber past fishing boats bow to stern all the way from Grimsby, and the old paddle steamer carrying passengers to and fro across the Humber and the old wooden wharves that must be long gone by now, but they smelt of fish and tar, reeking of a hundred years of sweat and toil when the sun was out, and quiet Sundays in Pearson Park where old men in white shirts and braces played bowls in the shade under the trees, the measured strides of men past seventy and the far-off clicks when the wooden bowls collided. It was so quiet you could hear your watch tick and your heart beat. And old Abrahamsen was young and lay on the grass kissing Mona O'Finley from Dublin. Her father had fled Ireland after 1916 and settled in 14 Pendrill Street, a grey house in a row of grey houses, off Beverley Road heading east. Oh, he liked Hull all right, there was not much of an upper class there, and on some days all you could hear around the harbour was Danish and Norwegian. And if talking to your neighbours was not what you fancied, you could go and have a pint at the Polar Bear, the finest pub in the world, where men in faded blue clothes were discussing trade union politics and poetry.

'Oetry?'

'Yes, for sure, poetry, and if you ask me, that was the best time of *my* life. You know, Audun, there are so many things in this world. It's not just here and now.' I nod, and we pass through the Sinsen intersection and up the hills past Aker Hospital to Bjerke trotting stadium at the top, and I really wished we would never get to Veitvet.

16

I am off sick for the rest of the week and the whole of the next. My mother's got a cleaning job at the Park Hotel, so she is away for most of the day, and I drift around the flat on my own, curtains drawn, drinking soup through a straw and lying in bed, reading and taking painkillers whenever I have to. At six she comes home and tells me the latest news about celebrities and pop groups staying at the hotel, about their drinking and the state of the rooms and toilets after they've left. She is ruthless. I miss talking with Arvid, but he doesn't ring me, so I don't ring him.

The Sunday before I return to work, I go for a walk in Østmarka. I take the Metro from Veitvet to Tøyen and change there and go to Bogerud and walk into the woods from Rustadsaga. It's cold, the air is crisp and clear and dead leaves lie in golden heaps along the hiking trail. My body still feels sore, but it's working again, and I push the pace until the muscles tell me it's enough. It is good to breathe after many days indoors. I have changed the large plaster for a smaller one, so I don't have a snub nose any more. The swelling has gone down, and apart from a few yellowish-blue marks and the plaster, my face looks almost normal. I have a cigarette in my pocket. I am going to smoke it when I'm halfway. I don't meet anyone that I know. People from Veitvet trek in Lillomarka.

And I don't see any animals, but long Lake Elvåga is glittering in the sunshine. About halfway, I stop and slide down and sit on the slope by the bank. It is fine and open here, and the trees are naked. I take out the roll-up and a little notebook I like to think is similar to the one that Hemingway used in the Twenties in his Paris book *A Moveable Feast*. I light the cigarette and try to do what he did: write one true sentence. I try several, but they don't amount to any more than what Arvid calls purple prose. I give it another go, and try to get down on paper the expression on Dole's face when I dragged him by the leg across the floor of Geir's bar. It's better, but not very good. I leave it for the day and put the notebook back in my jacket pocket and clamber up to the path. I go north along the lake to Elvågaseter restaurant. I order a coffee and sit by the window. I let the coffee cool for a few minutes. I speak to no one. Then it's the last stretch, up past Vallerud to Gamleveien. There is a bus stop there. I have to wait for half an hour, but that's fine with me.

The bus is nearly empty, just an elderly man with a rucksack sitting at the very front talking to the driver. I sit at the back as I always do, thinking that for one and a half weeks I haven't spoken to anyone except my mother.

The next day, I'm back on late shift. I sleep in for as long as I can, and when I catch the Metro, I am wearing Abrahamsen's grey suit. It attracts attention. People stare in the Underground, and in the cloakroom at work there is whistling and polite bowing between the cabinets. Trond waves his arm and says I look like something straight out of a black and white film from the 1930s, and others say, hand on heart, that the tapered trousers are what make the greatest impact. The suit causes so much of a stir that no one mentions my face. Which was pretty much the idea.

Jan is off sick again. He has been sent to hospital. No one talks about what may be wrong with him. He is the paper roll man, and I have been trained as his substitute. Trond winks and says promotion is just round the corner. Trond is supposed to step in on the paper-folder, but the man there is never ill. A change is welcome, and I must work alone, which I like, but it's a lot more hectic.

The rolls of paper are stored on a large platform, row upon row in the next room. Each of them weighs a ton, and they are transported on a little trolley that runs on rails from the platform to the middle of the press where the roll star is. There is room for three rolls in the star. My job is to keep it filled and not *ever* lag behind, and the art of it is to make the splice. The paper is spliced when the press is going full blast, and so I need a length that matches the speed. I calculate the angle and make a V-shaped tear along a steel ruler and fix the tip back against the roll and cover it with a precise pattern of strong double-sided tape. When the old roll is almost finished, I swing the star 120 degrees round until the new roll is straight under the web and start up the motor until it's running at the same speed as the rest of the press. And so I stand waiting, waiting, my finger on the button, and then I have to push it, and a brush pastes the join to the paper web and a knife cuts off the old roll with a bang. The sport is to get as close to the cardboard

168

core as possible. If all goes well the splice is removed at the folder, and if it *doesn't*, there is a howl and the paper comes streaming out of its web, or it concertinas, and we have to stop the press and re-thread the whole web. That takes an hour at worst, with test runs and washing down, and I am no one's favourite. It doesn't always go well, but I am not stupid, and Jan has been a good teacher.

Today all goes well. I toil and sweat and enjoy my work, I kick-start the trolley and stand on it as I shoot along the rails into the next hall, cut off the wrapping, and manoeuvre the paper rolls to the edge of the platform and rock them gently on to the trolley. There's a trick to it: if I push too hard the roll topples over, and that's why I wear my steel-toed shoes. They are supposed to take a ton's weight, but I don't feel like testing the claim. I keep the star full and two rolls in reserve, and by lunchtime not one splice has gone awry.

In the canteen we play cards, printers and assistants at their separate tables; this is lunchtime apartheid, but I couldn't care less. Everything's gone better than expected. When Trond suddenly looks at my face and asks what I was really up to last week, I just answer with a shrug.

Goliath and the other printers are sitting at the next table. Midway through lunch, Jonny goes to their table from his corner and takes a seat. They deal him in, but he makes so much noise and laughs so hysterically that they send him off with a flea in his ear, and he has to go and sit down on his own again. I keep a watchful eye on him.

'How's Jonny doing?' I say. Trond peers over his cards towards the corner.

'Much worse. Every day he picks a quarrel with the foreman and turns up late every other. He's on the edge. I've got a tenner on him to blow his stack this week. I don't think I'll lose.'

Neither do I. Jonny sits chewing on his sandwich and stares out the window, but outside there is nothing to see, it's pitch black. I have an urge to go up and talk to him, but then I don't. He is not in my league.

After the break, he runs around Number Three yelling at everybody and getting more and more desperate, and then he is off to the cloakroom. This keeps happening, and each time he returns with his body in a knot and throws himself at the ink regulators, but now he is the one making mistakes. His team is at their wits' end, they have to stop the press every half an hour to re-set.

There's a web break on ours. It's not my fault, but Harald, who is Elk's deputy, is running around giving orders and has fingered me as the sinner. He is sweating. I'm not afraid of him, I know what I am doing, and I do it my way, so I just turn my back on him. Goliath stands watching with a wry grin. I have no idea whose side he is on. We never talk. We prise out all the fragments that got stuck, and Goliath starts the machine on slow, and we thread a new web and wash down the blankets. It's no problem, we are ahead of schedule. Harald can do his job, and I can do mine. When the press is running, I stock up with rolls, make the splices on the two already in the star and take out my pack of Petterøe and roll a cigarette. If all goes as it should do, I have twenty minutes.

First I tidy up around my post, chuck the rags soaked

with white spirit in the red bin and throw all the other junk in the waste container. Then I take out a book from my bag and go behind the machine and sit down on a stack of pallets and open it. Right in front of me, the large double door is open to the next hall. The presses have been going all day, and it's hot. Behind me, Samuel is standing at the belt taking the folded sheets out of the stacker, and then he works them on the vibration plate and lays them on the pallet. He is singing aloud to himself with his earplugs pushed well in. I try to catch what it is he's singing, but he must have made up the song himself, because it's like nothing ever known to the human race. I read and smoke and take an occasional look into the next concourse. Everything is running and humming. Jonny is standing by the console on Number Three with his finger on the button pushing up the speed. He is way behind schedule and will have trouble with management if he doesn't deliver. Suddenly the paper flies, there is a bang and it catches fire. Jonny leaps screaming into the air, and his team run up the stairs to the gallery to put the fire out, and I put my book down, it is ten minutes past nine, and Jonny lets loose an ear-splitting howl that cuts through the drone of machinery, it's like an animal's scream, and he grabs a pallet, he is a discus thrower now, Jonny so small, the pallet so big, but it takes off, it takes off like a flock of sparrows through the hall and crashes against the foreman's window, it's like the sun lighting up a shower of glass, and then everything grows quiet, even though the other presses are still working. Now he's a goner. I close the book and start to run.

I get there at the same time as the foreman: he is out of

his office looking petrified, and I come from the opposite direction. I get there first, push in between the foreman and the press and block his path and start picking up sooty paper and fragments of glass.

'Where's Jonny?' he says. I straighten up and feign a bewildered look. 'Jonny? Who's that? Does he work here?' I mutter under my breath, not knowing if he can hear me or not. With Jonny gone into thin air and the whole crew on the gallery, I just couldn't stand by and do nothing. The foreman casts around, but there is no one to talk to, so he turns to me, small bits of glass crunching under his shoes.

'What the hell are you doing in here?' he says. 'Why aren't you on Number Five where you belong?'

'There was a paper break here, so I thought I could give a hand.'

'Give a hand? You should be doing your own damn work!' He is losing it, everyone is looking away, and I realise he is not going to say anything about the window even though he is up to his knees in broken glass and I am the only person around. But I'm not going to back down now, and that makes me feel calm.

'I *am* doing my own work,' I say.

'What do you mean? Are you being insolent?'

'I am not being insolent.' I am just saying I do my work. No one can say any different.

'I'll tell you one thing, Sletten. I've been keeping an eye on you. You're a troublemaker, are you not?'

'You can call me whatever the hell you like, but you can't say I don't do my work.'

I crossed the line there. But this day started too well. I must have been an idiot to think it was going to last.

I drop what's in my hands and walk towards the hall, where I can see Samuel's back. He still stands singing and has not heard a thing. I start to count. When I get to five, the foreman shouts:

'SLETTEN!' I stop and turn round.

'YOU'RE FIRED! YOU CAN GO HOME, NOW!'

'Kiss my arse,' I say.

That was quick. I go in past Samuel, and my legs are trembling. There is air instead of bones inside them. It's a strange feeling. I can ask old Abrahamsen to help me get a job at the harbour. I am strong, I can lift sacks. I don't know. What is certain is that my mother will be beside herself. I walk past the soundproof room where Goliath is sitting by the console filling in today's log. He looks up as I pass. I don't look back, just go to fetch my book and then on to my place at the rolls star and put the book in my bag. The old roll will soon be empty. I could just go away and let it run out, but everything has been so perfect today, and no one can say I don't do my job, even if I don't have it any more. I go over and swivel the star round, start up a new roll and when it's up to the right speed, I let the splice go. It sticks. Davidsen, the foreman, can go hang himself. It's a little early to make a join if you want to save paper, but it's better than having the press run empty, and I don't want to wait. I want to leave now.

When the join has gone through the web and been taken

out at the folder, I grab my bag and walk along the press. Goliath looks up again, he sees the bag, he looks surprised and comes to the door.

'That join was a little early, wasn't it?'

'I didn't want to wait. I'm leaving.'

'Leaving? Hell, you've only just got here. You've been away for more than a week.'

'I've been fired.'

'What are you talking about? No one gets fired from my team without me being told about it.'

'Maybe so, but just the same, I was fired five minutes ago, by Davidsen.'

'Goddamnit. HARALD!' Harald comes running in with blue ink dripping from his spatula. He has been stirring one of the tubs, and now it's running down his trousers. 'YES?' he shouts over the drone of the machine.

'Stop the press. Nice and easy. And don't move a fucking finger until I'm back.' He heads for the door. Then he stops and turns to me.

'And you stay right here.'

'Don't make any trouble for my sake. I don't give a shit about Davidsen.'

'Sometimes you're such a fathead, Audun, it's painful to watch. If you gave a little less of a shit, maybe you would get on better. But I can't lose a good roll man because of some useless foreman. So you stay right here. Do you understand what I'm telling you?'

'Fine,' I say. 'Fine.' Goliath pulls up his shoulders and rushes out the door, and the roar of the press subsides, the valves let out steam, and the web of paper goes white, and then it stops and it's quiet. Samuel looks up from his post by the stacker, he is still singing, and now I can hear what song it is, it's 'Johansen's Jumper'. Trond looks up from the book he is reading. He borrowed it off me, and I borrowed it off Arvid. He'll get it back, one day.

'What's that noise?' Trond says.

'It's Samuel singing.'

'Oh, shit.'

I stay at my post by the rolls star. This is just crap. I want to get out of here. You do it yourself, or you leave. That's the way it is, and I want to go.

'What's going on?' Trond says. 'Why have we stopped?' I shrug and stay there. I am the only person sitting. The others are standing, scratching their heads, and then Goliath and the foreman come in through the door. They are yelling at each other. Goliath is waving his arms around as he walks towards the press. I grab my bag and stand up.

'Sit back down,' Goliath says. 'This is a fag break.' He fetches his chair from inside the soundproof room and places it right in the middle of the floor with his back to the foreman. The others do the same, and they sit down, take out their tobacco and roll cigarettes. Davidsen is the only person standing now, and his face is beetroot-red.

'Hey, Odd!' he shouts. 'Start the press now!'

Goliath lights his cigarette, inhales and blows out.

'Jesus, that was really wonderful,' he says. 'Today it's been one thing after another, I haven't even had the time to smoke a cigarette. We're spoiling management, that's what we're doing.'

'Odd! You heard what I said! I'm in charge here!'

175

No one can see him except for me. He is sweating, his white coat is too tight on him. He runs a hand through his thinning hair, and Goliath gets up and goes over to the press, pulls the spatula knife from his work pants and cuts the paper just above the star. Swish it goes! And then the two ends hang in the air. He puts the spatula knife in its pocket and sits down with his back to the foreman. Davidsen is close to crying. He looks at his watch. Very soon it will be too late to fire up. There won't be time enough to wash the press down and start afresh before the shift is over. His shoulders crumple.

'Audun, you'll do the splice. That's your job.'

'I don't work here,' I say.

'Don't try to be funny. Do as I tell you.' I look at Goliath. He nods. I get up from my chair and go over to the star and put it in neutral, pull the paper until I have enough to work with. Then I take out the sticky tape and make a strong join.

'OK, let's go,' Goliath says, and stubs out his cigarette. 'Get those blankets wet.'

Afterwards he comes up to me, 'Do you know what, Audun,' he says, 'you're a troublemaker.'

'At least I do my job,' I say, and then he smiles his wry smile. Maybe his mouth just is like that.

17

For three days it has been snowing, and then it turns bone cold. Everything is different, it feels warmer down the stairs to the rotary press, and when evening comes, the doors open, casting yellow shadows, and my footprints shine in the dark on my way home from the late shift. My body is tired in a different way, time passes, that's why, I know, and my mother doesn't play opera as much and watches more TV. There are times I miss Kirsten Flagstad and Jussi Björling, but Jussi is taboo now. My hands have cracked up, so the ink doesn't really wash off. Touching my shoulders and thighs is like rubbing stone, and then I think about what those hands might do to Rita's skin or even Fru Karlsen's, and I find some sticky mess in my mother's cabinet and smear myself with it. And yet there is a change I have been waiting for that doesn't happen.

I lie in bed under the duvet with only my nose out over the top and see the starry frost on the old windows. We were supposed to have changed them for a new kind, the ones you operate with a handle and tilt, but my mother didn't want to spend the money, and now she has fallen out with the neighbours who think it looks ugly and unsymmetrical. Before I've even considered getting out of bed, the telephone rings. I lie back waiting for my mother to answer it. She doesn't. The flat is completely silent apart from the shrill ringing tone that comes up the stairs and into my room. If only I had remembered to close my door last night, then perhaps I would not have heard it, but now it's too late.

I don't want to, and then I have to. I thump my fist on the pillow, thrust the duvet aside, jump out and run downstairs in my underpants only, knowing the phone is bound to stop the second I pick it up. It always does. But it keeps ringing, and I grab the receiver and shout into it: 'Yes, hello, what *is* it?'

'Jesus, you got a hangover?' It's Arvid. I am frozen, I cover one foot with the other and try to make myself as small as I can, but I am one seventy-eight tall and practically naked.

'Shit, don't you know the working class have a right to weekends off? By the way, this is a rare honour.'

'And the same to you. Anyway, you're not supposed to rest, you're supposed to work the time you're on this earth. You must seize the day and the hour, you have to go skiing with me in the woods. The snow is great, and I need some air. Imagine a Kvikklunsj chocolate bar and cocoa in Lilloseter or Sinober.'

At least he's trying. And I think: come on, Arvid, and say:

'Sinober's too far. And I haven't had my skis on for two years. I don't even know where they are. Isn't it damned cold?'

'Don't forget Ingstad out on the tundra. In the mornings he had to thaw the dogs over the fire. That was cold. Minus fifteen is more like a sauna. Find your skis, you've got them in the cellar, I know you have. See you out by the military camp in an hour. Green Swix is good for waxing. Goodbye.'

He hangs up, and there is only silence. I stand listening. Where is my mother? I go upstairs and knock on her bedroom door, and when she doesn't answer, I open it. The room is empty, the bed's been made. I look at my watch. It's just nine o'clock, and it's a Sunday, and then the telephone rings again. I'm still half naked, every room is cold, and I curse and have to go back downstairs.

It's Kari.

'Is Mamma there?' She says *Mamma*.

'No, in fact she's not, I don't know where she is. I've just got up. The telephone keeps ringing, I'm standing here stark naked, and I'm freezing my arse off.'

'Audun?'

'Yes.'

'I want to come home, Audun. I don't want to spend Christmas here. I want to come home.' She whispers the last words. 'I think I have to hang up,' she says quickly, and then it's the dialling tone. I stand with the receiver in my hand, listening, and all I hear is the beep.

'Kari?' I say before I even start thinking, and then I slam the receiver down and go upstairs to my room and search for clothes. I find a thick jumper and a pair of old skiing pants at the back of the wardrobe and red knee socks. Then I go down to the kitchen and put the kettle on for coffee. Where did I last see the ski wax? I go to the worktop and pull out drawer number two under the cutlery and there they are: small tins of red, blue and green Swix. In the country it was always the firewood box we rummaged through, when something went missing, and here, when the odd item disappears, it ends up below the cutlery in drawer number two. The skis are on the fire escape outside the kitchen window, I suddenly remember. They have been there for two years. I pick up the green Swix, hold it in my hand, weigh it, and then I see the photograph of Kari with her newborn baby on the wall above the kitchen table. I put the tin back, close the drawer and go out into the hall and dial Arvid's number. He picks up.

'Hi,' I say. 'Is your father there?'

'My father?'

'Yes, your father. Can I have a word with your father?'

'Christ. OK. Don't go away.' He puts down the phone, and I hear him walk into the living room and call up the stairs, and then all goes quiet, and after a couple of minutes a door is shut, and Arvid's father says:

'Hello?'

'Hello, it's Audun. I know this is a little over the top, but I have to ask. Would it be possible to borrow your car for two or three hours today? It's my sister in Kløfta. I think there's a crisis, and I need to go. The bus takes too long. I'll be careful. Word of honour.'

'Well, actually I was going to use it myself today, but I suppose it can wait. It's important, you say?'

'I think it is. It would be cool of you. I have no one else to ask.'

'Then you'd best be going right away.'

'I'm already there. Thank you very much.'

I guess a reefer jacket and red knee stockings is not the latest fashion, but there is no time to change, and I lock the door as I leave. Wherever my mother is, she has her own key. And then I remember the kettle on the stove and have to go back in. I hurry through the hall, and in the kitchen I pull the kettle off the hotplate and close the lid with a bang. I start to sweat under my jacket by the stove and remember that this was the day I had planned to stay in bed and just take things one after the other. I slice off a chunk of brown bread before I leave and chew on it as I lock up and hurry along the Sing-Sing gallery.

I come out of the tower at ground level and run in the snow between the houses and across Veitvetveien. There are two cars stranded by the kerb with their iced-up windows and starter motors sounding like bad attacks of bronchitis as the drivers inside twist the keys. The frosty mist from my mouth fans out in the air, and coming down Veitvetsvingen, I see Arvid standing on the road by the car with the key dangling from his mitten.

'If there's a crisis, I'll go with you,' he says.

'Sorry about the skiing trip.' I rub my ears, there is an ice-cold wind, as there always is, and I haven't worn a cap for years.

'No problem. At least I'll get some fresh air, I'll just roll down the window.'

'Oh no, you don't.'

We pull the grey tarpaulin off the car. It is unwieldy and stiff, and when we fold it there is a cracking noise, and with a struggle we force it into the boot. The windows are ice-free, and the car starts first time. There is no nonsense with Frank Jansen's car.

'You can tell your father I'll pay for the petrol.'

'He'd expect nothing less,' Arvid says.

We drive round the bend and along Grevlingveien towards the shopping centre and then up to Trondhjemsveien. I switch on the heating and the fan starts humming, and then there is a smell of something burning, and only very slowly does the car thaw out. We keep our mittens on. The road is nearly empty, only the occasional lorry steams past, and then we are lost in a spray of snow, and I have to cut the speed to keep the car on the road, and then suddenly the road gets all slippery, and I really have to concentrate.

Driving with your mittens on is difficult. My hands slip on the steering wheel and I clench them so hard my whole body goes tense, and my neck feels so stiff I can hardly turn my head. We drive without speaking. Everything out there is white, but the roads have been cleared, and the trees that glide past bristle with rime and crystallised snow. I give up on the mittens, pull them off, and the wheel is cold and damp against my palms, and we can see the white smoke curling upwards from the chimneys on every rooftop. We drive past Grorud, with the church, and the school down in the valley, and Lake Stemmerud up in the woods, where we used to swim in the summer. I almost drowned there once, but then it was thirty degrees plus. I was diving and hit my head on the bottom and didn't have the strength to swim ashore, so instead I crawled along the bottom until my lungs were screaming. It was just my luck I didn't crawl the wrong way. It was so embarrassing I didn't tell anyone.

Arvid says nothing until Gjelleråsen Ridge:

'Is it a serious crisis, you think?'

'James Dean is no good. I've told them all along, but no one will listen. I don't get what a great bird like Kari's doing with him. Maybe we have to do a little kidnapping. Are you up for it?' I try to laugh, but it's not funny.

'I'll do whatever you tell me. You're the boss on this one.'

'Maybe there is no problem. But, whatever happens, Kari and the baby are coming with us when we drive back. Kari's always been OK with me.'

'So you owe her, is that it?'

I shrug. 'She's my sister,' I say. 'Call it what you like.' Arvid is about to answer, and then he doesn't and looks away and says to the window:

'Sorry. Stupid thing to say.'

Yes, it was, but I can't think about that now. Behind my eyes there are images flashing, making it hard to see straight. My hands tingle, and heat wells up inside me, and inside the car the windows are freezing up, until finally I can't see a thing. Arvid takes an ice-scraper from the glove compartment, but the humid air freezes and clogs the windows faster than he can remove it, and I have to pull over, roll the windows down and then we both scrape the windscreen. I look at my watch again, this is taking too long.

'Jesus, haven't you finished yet?'

'Take it easy,' Arvid says. 'We'll have to drive for a while with the windows down, I guess. The fan's not the greatest in the world.' He scrapes the windows clean on the inside,

and I do the outside. I kick at the snow and check my watch
and say:

'OK, let's get the hell out of here.'

I drive through Gjerdrum to Ask with the windows open,
it's cold as hell, and from Ask I cut across to Kløfta,
towards Ånerud. That's where his place is. I have been there
only once, for the christening, but I remember exactly
where it is, I remember JD on the steps with the baby in
his arms, the proud father, and Kari, pale and worn in the
background.

I turn just before the Shell station and look at Arvid. He
is quiet and serious.

'Do you remember the last time we were here?' I say. 'At
least this time we've got enough petrol.' The petrol gauge
is at three-quarters full. He smiles, but says nothing.

'Do you regret coming with me?'

'Hell no, it's not that. Of course I want to come with you.'
That's about all he has to say, and I do not ask, I have to keep
my mind on the driving. The road goes up hill and down
dale out here, and there are sudden bends, and even though
the road has been cleared, it's still slippery and churned up.
We round a bend, and I concentrate so hard on what's straight
ahead of me that I miss the driveway. I don't have time to
slow down, so I brake instead, and skid sideways past the
gate and come to a stop crosswise on the road some twenty
metres further down. There is no one else around, only the
engine is humming, and Arvid looks at me.

'No problem,' I say, wrenching the wheel hard. There is

just enough space to coax the car straight, and it's back and forth a hundred times, but I make it in the end, and then I slowly drive up to the gate and switch the engine off. We sit looking at the house. It's quite a large house for two adults and a baby. Once upon a time the house was dark, built with tarred boards perhaps, and then later he might have made a half-hearted attempt to paint it white, and given up after one coat, and the brownish tar is showing, and now the paint is flaking off and the house looks weary. On the drive there are two snow-covered vehicles: the lorry I have seen before and a Ford Mustang, and there are no footprints or wheel tracks in the snow. To the right, at the back, is a woodshed. As far as I can make out, there are no tracks leading up to it. Inside the house, the curtains are drawn. No smoke from the chimney. It all looks cold and abandoned.

'Hell, there's no one here,' Arvid says.

'We'll see about that.' I get out of the car and slam the door so hard you can hear it from miles away, and I wade in through the gate and halfway to the house. The snow is up to my ankles. I stop and stare at the curtains in the window on the first floor.

'KARI!' I shout. My voice cracks in the freezing air and falls in splinters over the drive, there is a tinkling sound, like glass. I just know someone is standing behind the green flowery curtains.

'KARI!' I shout again. My back starts to itch, and I have this fleeting feeling that I have stood like this before, a long time ago, and then I remember when and decide I will not run off a second time and leave Kari behind. But from the house there is not a sound. I walk slowly towards it. A saw and a crowbar stand up against the porch. I pick up the crowbar and feel the frost tear at my palm.

'Audun!' I turn. Arvid has opened the car door. He's getting out, he looks at me and points to the crowbar and shakes his head. 'Drop that damned thing!' he shouts, but I hold the metal tight in my hands, and then the child is screaming inside the house. There is a pain in my chest, and I hunch around that pain. I smash the crowbar against the porch, sending a sharp, crisp report into every room, a dry twig snapping in the cold, a gunshot. There is something about that sound. I raise the crowbar, I am about to strike again, I am ready now, I will smoke him out if I have to, and the door swings open, and Kari comes out in her red coat with a large sheepskin bag in her arms. The baby is all wrapped up, I can't see its face, but I can hear the little whimpers from deep inside, and then Kari stops, rocking the bag gently and says:

'There, there, little one, everything's fine,' and I stand with my arm still in the air, I don't know what to do with it. I squint so hard my eyes start to ache, and I stare into the dark behind her.

'Where's James Dean?' I say. The words feel sluggish and stiff in the cold.

'James Dean?' Kari is puzzled, she looks up at the crowbar and then at me and bursts out laughing. 'Oh, Audun, that's so like you. You mean Alf. He's gone to Eidsvoll. He's been there for two days. He had some cars to buy.'

'But why did you ring, then?' I lower the crowbar like some alien thing I try to make invisible, but I have cramp in my forearm, and my hand feels numb and maybe it's frozen fast to the metal. Kari follows my every move, and she's no longer smiling.

'I told you, didn't I. I want to come home. What exactly were you going to do with that crowbar, Audun? Demolish the house? The door was open, I heard the car come and saw you from the upstairs window,' she says, pointing, 'and I just had to dress little one. She didn't want to be dressed, of course, so she cried like a stuck pig, but that's how it is. She hates that bag. Here,' she says, handing me the whole bundle. I have to drop the crowbar, it makes a clanking sound on the doorstep, and I take the bulging bag and hold it with numbed fingers. The baby starts to cry at once, and I stand there breathing smoke signals.

'Rock her then, Audun,' Kari says. And I rock away and hear Arvid coming up behind me.

'Hi, Arvid,' Kari says, 'I just have to fetch a few things. I didn't know you two would be here so quickly. When I had changed this little cry-baby, I rang you back, Audun, but you must have left already.' She turns and goes into the house. The door makes a creaking sound, and just before it bangs shut, a cat comes shooting out. Arvid rounds me like a buoy and throws himself at the cat, and he catches it and rolls around in the snow, wrestling as if the animal were ten times bigger, howling like Johnny Weismuller in the movies. After a short struggle he gets up, holding the cat firmly by the scruff of its neck. He is all white with snow and has a scratch on his cheek, the cat's wriggling and hissing, and Arvid raises a clenched fist and grins.

'I've got a brilliant idea,' he says. 'Why don't we kidnap

the *cat*! Then at least we'll have accomplished something. What do you think?'

I hear what he's saying, he is trying to be funny, but I don't really get it. I go on rocking the baby and I say, 'It's fine by me.'

He lets go of the cat, it's running before it hits the ground and rounds the house and is gone behind the woodshed. Arvid brushes snow off his clothes, sighs and looks up at me.

'Do you know something, Audun. Nothing's fine by you. Absolutely nothing. And you can stop rocking that baby, she's not crying any more.'

It's true. All around us, it is quiet; in the woolly bag, it's quiet. I look between the blankets and see the baby sleeping, her little face so smooth.

'I guess she's sleeping,' I say. Arvid nods, rubs his bare hands, takes the mittens from his pocket and puts them on.

'Shall I hold her for a bit? You could do with a breather.'

'No, no, I'm fine.' He nods again, wipes his nose with the mitten and takes a deep breath you could hear for miles and looks up into the air.

'Jesus, I feel like singing,' he says, 'I really do. But maybe I'd better not. She might wake up again.'

'Best if you don't,' I say. The door creaks, and Kari comes out carrying two large bags. She puts them on the step and locks the door with a huge key, and I hand her the baby, and Arvid goes over and takes one bag, and I take the other, and we wade across the drive to the car.

'That's all I could carry,' Kari says. 'It's mostly for little one. Alf will bring down more whenever he comes home. He knows I'm going. I said I had to get away for a bit, and then he started to cry. You want to get divorced, he said. Christ, we aren't even married.'

We push the bags down on the tarpaulin in the boot, and Kari puts the bag with the baby beside her on the back seat. Arvid and I sit at the front. I turn the key and start the car. Kari looks out of the window at the house.

'The old house. Shit, I think it's haunted, for a fact. Ride on, my gallant knight, and don't spare the horses. I want to go home!' Arvid laughs, and Kari laughs, and I coax the car gently up the slope, and then we glide along between the white fields towards Ask. The sun is out and shines as best it can, and the lines turn soft and yellow, and red in some places, and blue where the fields cut down to the river, and I think of what's there beneath, the frozen, the rigid, and we don't speak, and the baby is sleeping in the bag, and by the time we reach the Skedsmo junction, my hands are trembling so badly I pull into the verge, stop and say:

'How about taking over, Arvid?'

'I thought you'd never ask.' He opens his door, and I open mine, and we walk around the car. In front, by the grille, his shoulder gently brushes mine as he passes, and then we get in. I lean back in the seat, Arvid turns the car back on the road. I close my eyes. I could sleep now, I think, and then I fall asleep.

I don't wake up until we pull off Trondhjemsveien. In the bend, the low sun is straight in my face. It's not even noon yet, and I miss my old sunglasses, but I haven't worn them outdoors since I started training. Arvid drives under the

Metro bridge, into Beverveien, right by the big garage and down the hill. In front of the block, he parks the car with its nose well on to the footpath. Sore and stiff we get out of the car, Kari with the baby in her arms, and Arvid opens the boot, and I pick up one bag and lead the way. There is a Sunday silence in the stairway tower and along the Sing-Sing gallery, and when I enter our flat, my mother is sitting by the kitchen table, smoking, her forehead against the window.

'Hey, where were you?' I say. She looks at me, but her mind is miles away. She was never like this before. There is a silence, she is looking right through me. She takes a puff of her cigarette, slowly blows the smoke out and seems to vanish in it.

'I'm getting married again, Audun,' she says.

I put down the bag and wipe my hands on my trousers. The lid on the stove is up and the cylinder hotplate is reeking heat into the room.

'Who to? The man with the white back?'

'The man with the white back?'

'Forget it. Do I know who he is?'

'I wouldn't think so,' she says calmly, 'I haven't known him that long.'

'Aha. Are you going to move house then, or were you thinking that he should live with us?'

'That was the idea, yes,' she says, and now her mind is sharp. She sends me a defiant look.

'I see. Well, then it's going to be goddamn cramped here,' I say, and Kari comes in through the door, the baby is awake, and she calls through the hall:

'Hi, Mamma! Guess who's here!'

18

My father is dead. Two dog sledders found him on their way home from Lilloseter. It was the 22nd of December. They had taken a trail off the floodlit ski track and had seen a cabin in a clump of trees with a metre of snow on its roof. The cabin wasn't there before, they said, so they steered the dogs off the trail to take a closer look. They were young men of my age with red anoraks and that Helge Ingstad look in their eyes and blue and white Oslo Dog Sledders Club badges on their arms. The cabin was small and solid and as tight as a bottle. The person who had built it knew what he was doing. Inside the cabin my father lay in his sleeping bag on a mattress of spruce with a primus stove up by his shoulders. There was no paraffin left. He must have fallen asleep, and it had burned with a flame turning brighter and brighter and finally poisoned him. He didn't feel a thing. At least that's what the doctor at Aker Hospital said. He had been dead for three days, he said, but it was cold, and I could picture the grey-blue air and the snow with its hard crust and the dog sledders doing what they had to do with a lump in their throats, loading my father on to the sled as stiff as a board, and fast as a train they set off for Ammerud where they could ring for an ambulance. From some papers he kept in the grey rucksack, they found their way to us, and now I am glad they did.

The telephone call came at ten o'clock on the morning of Christmas Eve. I didn't know if I should laugh or cry. My mother was at the kitchen worktop rubbing salt and pepper into the pork to have it ready for the afternoon. Kari was out walking with little one. Alf had been down a couple of times, but Kari did not want to go back up, not yet anyway, and my mother didn't seem too unhappy about that. She liked being a young, active grandmother. Now we were just waiting for the next one to move in.

And then the phone rang in the hall. I pretended not to hear it, so she had to leave the kitchen, and she lifted the phone with two fingers and placed it between her chin and shoulder, flapping her hands covered with fat and spices. I could smell it from where I was sitting on the steps reading *Sailor on Horseback*. That's Irving Stone's biography of Jack London. Jack had just sold his first story to *Overland Monthly*. It was the hard work that won him the victory, and in that way a triumph, because it was something he could do. Work hard. His friends bought up the whole print run, but he received no more than five dollars for the story, and even I thought that was lousy pay, and then my mother went all quiet and just stood there with her hands still in the air and her mouth frozen into a half-smile, and I sat watching her instead of reading the book. I guess I knew what she was going to say before she said it. That's how it is sometimes. She put the receiver down with the same two fingers, very carefully, her eyes shiny and blank and bewildered.

'It's your father, Audun,' she said. 'He's dead. I can't fathom it. They said he was found dead in a cabin up in the woods here. I don't understand a thing, really I don't.'

I sat perfectly still, waiting. I never told her I'd seen him, only about the accordion and where it came from, and Kari had also kept quiet. I hadn't planned to tell her at all, but I felt sorry for my mother just then. She ran her sticky fingers through her hair, and then there were streaks of pepper and brown fat in her blonde locks.

'You're getting pork fat in your hair,' I said, but she wasn't listening, she stroked her hand across her face, and it left dark stripes on her cheek. It looked like warpaint.

'I have to go to Aker Hospital to identify him. I could wait until after Christmas, but I'd rather do it now and get it over with. The funeral and all that will have to be sorted out. I don't know how. You'll come with me, Audun.'

'No way,' I said. She looked at me then, in her new way. I didn't like it. I stood up, and Jack London fell and slid down the stairs, the stout photograph in black and white on the jacket knocking against the rails. The book belonged to Arvid's father, they never ran out of stuff at their place, and I bent down to save the cover, and as I stood up, I could see how angry she was.

'Oh yes you will!' she said. 'It's your father, for God's sake!'

'Hell, I don't have a father,' I mumbled, and I meant it, but then she was towering over me, unbending and hard, and she forced me up the stairs, step by step, grabbing my hair.

'Now we've both got pork in our hair,' I said, but she was deaf in that ear.

'I am not doing this on my own, Audun. You're eighteen years old and a grown-up now, and you've seen worse. If I can do this, so can you.'

And of course she was right.

'Fine,' I said, 'I'll come with you. I can ring Arvid's father and ask if I can borrow his car. That'd be quicker.'

'That would be great,' she said and let go of my hair.

I rang and told him what had happened, and he listened quietly until I had finished the story. I was starting to like the man, and then he said:

'That's fine, Audun. You just come and get it. I'll leave the key in the car, so all you have to do is drive off. But forgive my asking, what's up with you lot?'

'I don't know,' I said. 'I don't know what's up with us. Things just are what they are.'

'Well, fine then, you give my regards to your mother and tell her Happy Christmas and all good wishes.'

'Thank you,' I said.

It's not far to Aker Hospital. We drove ten minutes down a very quiet Trondhjemsveien, and of course it *was* him. I never doubted it. What my mother was thinking, I do not know, but there we were, standing in front of the steel table with his body on it, looking at the white face, and neither of us had really seen it for more than five years. We didn't cry, and I don't know why we should have. My mother gave the man in the white coat a nod and said yes, that is Tormod Sletten, and then she leaned over my father and stroked his hair.

'You were a stylish man. No one can take that away from

you,' she said, and turning to me, she said, 'You're starting to look like him, Audun, but of course, you've got my hair. There's no denying that.' She smiled and stroked my hair, too, and my cheek, and then it got a little awkward. Luckily she started talking to the white coat about the funeral, he could arrange it for the 29th he said, and I made for the wall and leaned against it and looked over at the table in the middle of the tiled floor. He was different now, his hair was grey, almost white, and his face was white, smooth even, and the furrows down his cheeks were not so distinct. Maybe they have done something to him, I thought, and carefully passed my hand over my own face.

As we left they gave us a bag with his personal effects. 'We had to confiscate the gun,' the doctor said. 'We searched through his things, but couldn't find a licence for it.'

'That's fine by me,' my mother said. She gave me the bag, and we walked along the corridors. We could hear our footsteps between the walls the whole way down, and there were red and green Christmas decorations hanging from every lamp, and on the door out there was a huge wreath with a bell. Back behind the wheel, I opened the bag and looked into it. There wasn't much: his knife, a few keys he had kept for long-forgotten doors, two fifty-kroner notes and a small black and white photograph. I picked it up, and the woman in it, I had never seen before. She had short, black hair and was sitting on a rock by a lake, maybe Aurtjern, the bay seemed familiar to me. *Marianne* it said on the back in his messy handwriting. I sat looking at the name, and then it came all the way back to me.

'Marana,' I said.

My mother leaned over the handbrake to study the photograph.

'Well, I never, that's Marianne Røkken,' she said. 'She was in my class at school. We were friends for a few years. She too fell in love with your father. I remember well when that photo was taken, because I was the one who took it. Fancy him carrying it around. That man!' She shook her head, and I looked more closely at the photo and realised it was the clothes that made her seem like a *woman*. She was probably no older than I am now. And it struck me that there were things in my mother's and father's lives that I would never get to know.

It was a strange Christmas Eve. When we came back from Aker Hospital, Kari was in the kitchen talking to Roberto. He had stopped by with presents and silly jokes, singing arias, and had just started a rendering of 'Jerusalem' that was the worst I had ever heard. He was making more noise than the four of us put together. I drew Kari aside and told her what had happened, and we agreed not to tell what we'd known the last few months. There was enough going on already.

At last the roast pork was in the oven. The aroma spread slowly up to the first floor and mingled with the sauerkraut and the burning candle wax, and the dead man's name was never mentioned. At three o'clock I watched Disney's Christmas programme as I always do.

Last year there were only the two of us at the table, and I cannot deny it felt a little dreary. This time the table was crowded: Kari sitting with her little one, and Alf had come down to be with his daughter on Christmas Eve, he was loaded with presents, but we were not impressed, and Olav, my mother's new boyfriend, rang the doorbell at five sharp. He brought plastic bags almost bursting at the seams and was visibly nervous. I decided to be nice and shook his hand. That helped a little, he started to relax, and my mother giggled and gave me a hug. He wasn't exactly my type, pretty plump all round and almost bald, but his arms bulged under his shirt, and when he smiled he even looked a little bright. I asked him if he read books, and he said he liked Mikkjel Fønhus. That was fine with me, I had read a few myself, and they were not bad. He was a printer at Aas & Wahl and after a few aquavits that gave us enough to talk about. But watching my mother shimmy round the table, sweaty and smiling as I'd never seen her smile before, I knew that there was only room for one of us. Then and there I decided to pay old Abrahamsen a visit, once this weekend was over. He had a spare room, and maybe he could use the extra money.

And then the 29th comes around. At Grorud Cemetery, the gravedigger has been thawing the ground for two days. I get up at the crack of dawn and start reading *The Apache Indians* by Helge Ingstad. Arvid gave it to me for Christmas. It's a nice-looking edition from Gyldendal's travel series, which he stumbled across in a second-hand bookshop, and there are several dedications on the inside leaf as well as the one to me. One of them says: To Arvid from Minna,

Arthur and the boys. He liked that, and we have made up stories about who these people might be. But it's hard to concentrate even though Ingstad could really write. It's dark outside, and I can hear Olav snoring in the room next to mine, and my mother talking in her sleep. It drives me down to the kitchen. It's dark there, too. I light a few candles and open the lid on the stove, put water on for coffee and flick through the book until the water is boiling. Then I sit down at the table and smoke and drink coffee and watch the coming day. The smell is different, there is someone breathing in every room, I hear little one whimpering in the one next to the kitchen. Soon she'll be awake and crying. In the glow from the candles, I take out the photograph of Marianne and look at it. The face is familiar now. She is only eighteen years old in the photograph, and it's summer, and if I ever get to write anything solid and good, I will start with that photograph.

It's the same priest. I am sitting on the front bench and listen to him speak. This time we were prepared and told him as little as possible. He recognised us, and for a second there, he was lost for words, but I have to say he makes the most of it. He is a pro. My mother turns and winks at me and smiles wearily. I smile back. It's all so strange we don't know how to behave. She is sitting with Olav. It's difficult not to like him now. I never would have thought he'd show up here. Kari is sitting beside my mother, rocking the baby, and old Abrahamsen on the bench behind, wearing the suit I had given him back, and all of Arvid's family is here, and

Roberto, and not one of us cares in the least what the priest has to say.

In the cemetery it's all white between the gravestones, and the stones are white on top, and only the steaming pile of fresh soil by the new grave breaks up the idyll. We form a small procession as we walk down. The coffin trolley creaks in the snow, and there are cold candles and burnt-out torches after Christmas. Mild weather is on the way, I can feel it in the air, you could make snowballs now, and if I'd been a few years younger, I would have. We round a vast, vulgar monument put up for some rich family, and we are there. In a circle we stand around the grave, and the priest sings *Alltid freidig når du går* all alone. We hoist the coffin by the straps, and the sexton winds the crank handle until the coffin is lowered halfway into the grave, beside Egil's. There are more flowers than last time, it's like a goddamn party, and suddenly that seems so unfair, and then I start crying. Everyone turns, but I cannot stop. The priest looks at me, he smiles, he's pleased, I am on the right track, he always knew I would be. I'm sure he has prayed to God on my behalf. My mother comes over and puts her arm around my shoulders, and Arvid looks me straight in the eye with a grin. I'll take care of him later. I smile at my mother, but that only makes it worse. My chest feels tight, I sob aloud. It's so goddamn embarrassing, I hide my face in my hands so I don't have to look at Arvid, or any of them. Martin Eden would never have done that, I know, but, hell, I am only eighteen. I have plenty of time.

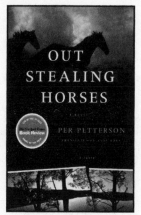

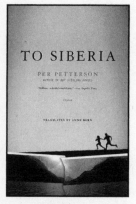
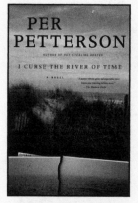